LOCK & KEY

Cyn Ley

LOCK & KEY by Cyn Ley
Copyright 2024
OTHERLAND PRESS

ISBN 978-1-7333859-9-2

Artist credits: Erika Milo

DISCLAIMER

This is a work of fiction. Names, characters, places and incidents are products of the author's imagination or used fictitiously. Any resemblance to events, locales, or persons living or dead, Is entirely coincidental.

ONE

Some things are just meant to be. Like an inevitable plot line.

Tim, college friend, best buddy, and now business partner, and I had decided to forsake the city lights in search of a place to set up shop.

Back then, it was just Tim and Joc, hitting the road and looking for adventure.

We'd met in college in a Modern Lit class, hit it off right away. I was a Lit Major and he was a Theater Major and the next thing we knew, we were untangling ourselves from abstract authors and I was helping him learn his lines. We discovered we both loved mysteries, and books, and the arts in general. We're best friends. There is no romance between us; we're just comrades in arms who thought we could make our shared interests lucrative and worked our asses off so we could buy a storefront and start a business.

We'd answered an ad, looking for a space to lease. It was out somewhere beyond the logic of the urban grids. Streets had names with no rhyme or reason, unless you and your folk had lived there for the past seventy years and knew that the road with the puzzling name of Franksnee was called that because seven-year-old Frankie Johnson had tripped over an old rusted railroad spike back in the 30's and given himself tetanus, and the family named the spot that in memory of him and the body part that took the hit.

We took a turn off the highway into a beautiful, forested area. The trees were thick and the effect a bit claustrophobic if your mind ran that way, which ours didn't. We were full of anticipation.

A few miles later, we emerged onto a charming main street, where rows of shops had adjoining walls and there wasn't a shopping mall in sight. They had timbered roofs and mullioned windows that looked out onto the street. Stained glass transoms crowned every shop door. Flower boxes adorned the entries and benches lined the walls. There were pedestrian thoroughfares, not sidewalks, and the streets were wide enough for two lanes of car traffic, neither to exceed 15mph. There was even a large town park nearby, set with picnic tables and gazebos and more flowers than you could take in in one glance.

It took our breath away.

We kept going, taking it all in. At the end of a row, a vacancy sign hung on a shop door, bearing a phone number. We peered in the windows. It was perfect. Going through the local paper, we even found a nice rental. The house was in good shape and big enough for both of us and our individual pursuits.

A few phone calls later, and just like that, we were home at work and play.

It was a good way to start the summer.

TWO

As we drove around the village, Tim suddenly sat up straight and pointed. "It's Fate!" he enthused. "Look there!"

I followed the track of his finger to a modest building, then drove up to it. A sign stood in front of it, a magic incantation written on it. "Community Theater" it read, and a broadside sheet was attached to it. "AUDITIONS FOR *PRINCES IN THE TOWER* BEGIN THIS WEEKEND. FOR MORE INFORMATION, CONTACT....", followed by a cell number.

I looked at Tim and deadpanned,

"Kismet, even."

He laughed.

So that Saturday afternoon, the two of us showed up at the appointed theater doors at ten o'clock sharp. Tim had gotten a copy of the play as soon as was humanly possible, and at this point had most of the male lead's lines memorized.

"That confident?" I asked. "Not that you're not good, but—"

"Go for the gold, get a part as a supernumerary," he said. "That's normal."

Tim had, as usual, understated his abilities. He's always had a passion for the stage and knew when he first stepped on one at aged six that this was where he wanted to be. He's a big believer in nurturing the arts in the community and has no inclinations or yearnings toward Broadway.

Not that he isn't good enough

though. He can sink into a character so deeply that even I have trouble sometimes remembering that Tim's in there. To top it off, he looks very Classical—tall and dignified, dark hair and a patrician nose and bearing. All he had to do is throw on an old scarf and everyone believes in that instant that he is Totally Upper Crust. His Lordship adjusts his silk ascot, bored and seemingly disinterested in the people and proceedings surrounding him, particularly those overly curious and annoying authorities.

A woman in her 30's appeared. She was auburn-haired, tall and slender, wearing beat-up jeans, a t-shirt spattered with paint stains, and holding a box cutter in one hand. I liked her immediately.

"That for us?" I asked, teasing.

She laughed and tucked it in her

pocket. "Come on in," she said. "You must be the new folks everyone's been talking about, the bookstore people?"

News traveled fast around here.

"That's us," Tim said cheerfully, and introductions were made all the way around.

"I do set design, props, make messes building and painting things, and am a serial killer of cardboard," Marion offered.

We chuckled. "Like mysteries, do you?" Tim ventured.

"Love them. Boy, have I got a list for you! You here for the auditions?"

"He is," I said.

"I act," Tim said. "Most recently, college productions. Theater major."

"That's wonderful," she said sincerely. "Peter's our director. Tall, blond, lives in T's, jeans, and sandals. He's really good. Has no interest in egos and full interest in art. He runs the theater department at the local high school. He's in the house—go ahead and introduce yourself."

As Tim scurried off, she turned and looked at me. "What about you?" she asked.

I am no actor, but I love art and am pretty good at it. If a new show is being designed, I'm right there in the thick of it. Tell me what you want, and I will give you one killer set, paintbrush in one hand and hammer in the other, thanks to my college experience. Here and now, our little community theater group does amazing work, and we all have a blast doing it, especially under Marion's capable direction.

I shared my college experience with her. "I've been told I'm pretty good," I said.

In return, she enthused, "Oh, we'll

keep you busy!", and the next thing I knew, this sparkling buoyant woman, clearly a force to be reckoned with, took me by the arm and brought me backstage and into her world of making magic. "So, what do you think?" she asked.

"I want to be a part of this," I said, and that sealed the deal on the start of what would become a lifelong friendship.

If Tim's claim to fame in our community was theater, mine was embroidery. I picked it up in high school and found it to be a wonderful way to express myself and relax at the same time. I've even won prizes with it, doing entirely original designs. Since moving here, I've contributed to town fundraisers and raffles, and apparently getting a Joc Peters piece is quite the prize. Shortly after we'd arrived, the town was having a fundraiser to repair the leaky library roof. I sat down with my pencil and sketched away. Six weeks later, the piece was done—children playing in a wonderland of children's books, with characters and scenes of the titles they represented. It's a big piece, measuring three feet by two feet without the frame. I set it in a simple wooden frame as the design was busy enough. Because we made it a point to attend as many of the monthly Council meetings as we could, I brought it—covered, of course—to the one before the raffle and asked if they would like it for the cause.

I love the sound of jaws hitting the floor.

The winner was one of the Councilwomen, who said she loved it and donated it to the library. Since then, it has held a place of honor over the checkout desk. It also brought in $850.

That Tim and I enmeshed ourselves in the community from the start ran in our favor. We soon went from being total strangers to knowing a lot of folks by name in no time flat.

THREE

Tim and I quickly got down to the business of setting up shop. While we found a number of pieces which worked admirably and affordably for our needs, most of the bookcases we found were just wrong—too tall, too short, too massive, too just not right. "Well," I said, "I suppose I could build some."

That took us down to the local hardware store, sketches in hand. We showed our drawings to Ed Graham, owner and manager, and one of the most affable people I've ever met. He knew his subject backwards and sideways and gave us more great advice than either of us could have imagined. Expressing our wonder, he just laughed and said that people are forever needing one widget or another. He also said that hardware stores are man caves, places for the local guys to shoot the breeze, kind of like sporting goods stores, and coming down in search of a widget was a good excuse to come down and do precisely that. Not that Ed was in any way sexist or demeaning—he was simply observant.

He also loved to teach and was good at it, never condescending. It's thanks to his know-how and various supplies that our bookshelves will never come loose. Ed taught me how to sink a butterfly screw with the best of them, and even Tim, who tried to take on this manly chore himself, got out of the way when I told him, "Outa my way, boy—let me

14

show you how a real woman screws."

He winced and let me alone after that.

Ed introduced us to Doug Lewis, who was out working the floor. I asked about finials, which we would use to decorate the top corners of our bookcases, and before we knew it, we were ready to start our builds.

We were about a week away from our scheduled opening and swamped. Taking a break and grabbing my cold espresso, I went and sat on the bench outside the door. Taking a long swallow, I lowered the cup, only to see a handsome teenage boy hurrying down the street, being led by two little fluffball doggos.

I am an absolute sap for dogs. Actually, for most animals, but dogs

come out on top. These two were
Bichons, cute as bugs, and the farthest
thing I've ever seen from the neurotic,
barky, snappy creatures that small dogs
can be sometimes. They looked bright
and happy, tails wagging, grinning as only
Bichons can. They were very friendly and
inquisitive, and one of the things they
wanted to inspect was me.

Stopping short, the kid spoke first.
"Hi, I'm Cam Lewis. My dad works at the
hardware store. He told me about you."

I raised an eyebrow. "Nothing too
scandalous, I hope! Hi. I'm Joc, one of the
owners here. My partner Tim is inside
fighting it out with a door lock."

Cam laughed. The fluffies pulled at
their leashes, trying to reach me. "Can
they meet you?"

"I'd be honored," I said. "I love dogs."

About two seconds later, they'd
jumped up on the bench with me and the

three of us were engaged in some meaningful dog-human conversation. Translated, I was being licked to death. "So, tell me about them."

It turned out that Doug had a fondness for armchair mountaineering and blindingly bad Dad jokes. He always said the dogs had pointy heads when they wanted to, meaning they'd take off where and when the whim hit them, and sometimes he swore that their little brains were oxygen deprived. Mountains and high altitudes just sort of ran together, as did the dogs. So he wanted to name them after famous peaks. While the family agreed that K2 was a cool name for a dog, Matterhorn was more problematic, too long and too subject to double entendres. "What's wrong with Matter?" Doug asked. "Everything matters!"

The family heaved a collective sigh

of resignation and agreed to call the dog Matt. So they became Matt in his blue collar and his trusty sidekick K2 in his green, which was pretty much the only way to tell them apart. Cam said they were brothers and shared one brain. Even so, they were quite smart and were well trained and obedient. K2 and Matt were the reason I kept a jar of small doggy biscuits behind the front counter and a water bowl at the ready.

But this particular day, I had already spent too much time malingering with Cam and the fluffies. "Excuse me," I said. "It's been a pleasure, but I really need to get back to work. We still have so much to do to make our opening."

Cam, I was about to learn, was a consummate opportunist. I liked that, especially in a teenager.

"Do you need some help?" he asked. "I know how to do a bunch of stuff--I've been working with Mr. Fokes for the school theater, and I help out at the community theater too."

My ears pricked up. "Tim!"

Before we knew it, we'd hired Cam at a reasonable rate for a couple of days and adopted two dogs who made us their second home. They often slept on the rug in the wintertime in front of the electric fireplace, or in front of the air conditioning vent in the summer and were as friendly and sweet to our customers as any dogs could be.

We all waited with bated breath for the final decisions on *Princes in the Tower*. When they were posted, I just looked at Tim. "Supernumerary, huh?"

FOUR

With Cam's help, we opened on time.

Our shop's name is "Lock & Key," subtitled "The Puzzler's Playground." We cater to those who love mysteries of all sub-genres, from cozies to literary stories, from the classic authors to the contemporary. All things inscrutable. We even have youth mysteries because kids love puzzles as much as adults do. And speaking of puzzles, we carry a very nice line of cards and games and jigsaws to keep you guessing and sharpen your sleuthing skills. It was a bit of a gamble, doing a bookstore that was so genre-specific, but there are shops which do nothing but sci-fi and others which focus on romance, so why not mysteries?

If you're coming up the row, we're easy enough to find. Last door on the right, if you please. You might take a moment to appreciate the Victorian-style sign hanging from the iron bracket outside the door, proclaiming the legend of "Lock & Key, Joc Peters and Tim Waverly, Proprietors" written beautifully in gilt on red. Inside, the Victorian theme continues, the era which saw the birth of the true mystery novel. There is a small comfy sitting area with three tall armchairs and small setting tables, crowned by a lovely Tiffany-style lamp. They are set in a U configuration around an Oriental rug, ringing the electric fireplace. As Holmesian as all that may sound, our customers tell us it's charming.

The building is older, but solid. We've occasionally heard critters under the storeroom ever since we moved in. Even though we have the exterminators come in every few months and make sure that all routes into the shop are inaccessible, we do hear them from time to time. Fortunately, we've never had any make it in.

This place used to be a ladies' clothing shop, and much to our delight, the two adjoining dressing rooms were left intact. We knocked out all the partial walls and added a heavy door that deadbolted. Just the right size for the files, a counter, some shelves, the safe, a mini fridge, a small microwave, and the absolute necessity of an espresso machine. In a small business like ours, it makes much more sense to do our receiving up at the front counter where we can be available to our customers.

The shop has a storeroom in the back, a little cubbyhole in the far inner corner. The door to it is covered by a heavy crimson Victorian-style drape. We put up shelves and keep our overstocks there. There are Victorian touches here and there, like the antiqued finials on the top ends of the bookcases, screwed there so they can't go walkabout. We installed a mail slot in the front wall, just behind a beautiful oak front counter that we restored ourselves.

We had a sign at the counter which read, "Do you have a favorite author? Series? Looking for something, old, rare, or unusual? Give us your requests!" We kept a running list. We carried both new and gently used out of print books, the classics and the contemporary, and were always happy to do a book search for anyone who asked. Like Tim's coffee, this service also proved to be quite popular. The hours were posted on the door. The place was cozy but not crowded. Everything looked and felt right.

We were ready.

We opened to a steady stream of customers that lasted all day. Tim and I had the espresso maker going, and everyone was welcomed with a small cup of his excellent brew. Nothing says "Pacific Northwest" like espresso!

True to her word, Marion showed up on opening day with her list of 15 titles. This was the start. "Told you." She laughed.

"I'll see what we can do for you, ma'am," I said, taking it from her. Some of the titles were quite obscure, but I loved the thrill of the hunt.

When we first opened, we were mobbed as the newest thing in town, which was to be expected. Happily, our instincts proved right. The shop started popular and has stayed that way, bringing in visitors from outside our little village, so that's been good for everyone.

Among our regulars was Doug Lewis, Cam's dad. He loved old-fashioned hard-boiled mysteries, and presented us with a list when he first came in. Then he told us about his wife Ellie. "She thinks she can write," he said. "I think she can too. She's got good ideas, but she can't write them into a story. She says it all gets mixed up in her head, and any publisher she's ever submitted to has always rejected her. I asked her to check you out—she's been meaning to anyway—but she's kind of embarrassed. There's only so much disappointment one person can take."

"It's a tough business," Tim said. "We haven't had the pleasure of meeting her yet."

"Oh, she'll be along," Doug said with a smile. "Just wait."

"Success in writing though--one never knows," I said thoughtfully. "Anything in particular?"

"Everything interests her. Maybe that's part of the problem."

When we first met Ellie, we understood why Doug felt like he did. Her mind was perfectly capable of going from petunias to quantum physics without skipping a beat, and she needed people who were willing and able to take that journey with her. We met a kind and fascinating woman and liked her from the very start. Ellie was one of those who could lead a reader down a multitude of pathways, including many that you'd never known were even there.

It seems that intrigue is one of those things which grabs you by the throat and then doesn't want to let go. Wherever you happen to find it.

FIVE

Marion stopped by. She was more or less dragging her unwilling ten-year-old son Johnny with her. She'd been anxiously awaiting her favorite author's latest and wanted to know the instant it showed. It had arrived today, been received into stock, a copy tagged for her. I texted her cryptically. "The Orient Express is in the station," I wrote.

She wrote back, "LOL. On my way. Just picked kid up from soccer practice. Thanks!"

A short time later, she bustled in the

door, Johnny scuffling behind her. "But Mom, I don't wanna be here," he complained. "I wanna go play."

"This will take five minutes," she said. She looked slightly worse for wear, the wind having blown her short hair all over the place. "We'll be home soon. Okay?"

"Okay," he said. He wandered off to the British Mysteries section, where he took various books off the shelves to look at the covers and read the backs. When he finished with one, he set it carefully on the floor, then moved to making short little piles. He wasn't hurting anything, but it still made me nervous.

I really wished Tim was here. He's great with kids, and sometimes puts on little performances for them from his favorite plays just for fun. The kids adore him. But today he'd needed to leave early—Peter had called the actors in for blocking, and I still had an hour before I could go.

I finished ringing up Marion's purchase, handed her back her change. "Would you like a bag?" I asked.

"No thanks." She smiled. "I'm going to have enough trouble trying not to read it while I'm driving home." She turned. "Ok, we're leaving now."

Her son made his way back, leaving several stacks of books on the floor.

Marion's eyes turned dark. Her voice low, she said, "Put those back where you found them. Now."

I've always called this "the Mother Voice." The voice that tells you that you are just barely this side of not dead.

Johnny realized that the shit had hit the fan, and he was it. He looked at his mom and confessed, "I don't know where they all go," he said.

His mother was no wimp. "Then pick

them off the floor and put them neatly on that table there. I believe you owe Ms. Joc an apology."

Johnny decided to deal with the books first. He picked them up carefully and set them in tidy short stacks.

He came up to the counter. "I'm really sorry," he said. "I wasn't paying attention."

"I know," I said. "I accept your apology. Just try not to do it again, okay?"

He nodded solemnly, and they left.

Sometime later, Johnny went out to play ball with some friends in the park.

As we would later learn, no one recalled seeing him there.

After work, Cam and I met at the theater to finish putting together the wall screens. We'd painted them earlier in the week—one blue side, one yellow—and now they were dry enough to finish. All we had left to do was install and paint the hinges. Marion's clever design gave us two adjustable backdrops for the price of one. Even unfolded all the way, the backdrops were quite easy to move and adjust as needed with two people. No matter how they were used, the whole metamorphoses took under a minute.

All we had left to do were the hinges. After we measured, matched and set the screws, we slowly opened and closed the panels a few times to check them for stability, smoothness of action, and absence of squeak.

Satisfied, it was time to get the hinges painted. We left the screens partially unfolded so they wouldn't wobble with our work. I tossed Cam a roll of masking tape and we carefully taped around the front and back of each hinge to minimize the risk of any paint going where it wasn't supposed to. Cam would do the blue side and I the yellow. I was rinsing our small brushes and pressing all excess liquid out of them when I heard him talking on his cell.

Peter allowed cell phones as long as conversations were kept under two minutes, and only when no actors were on stage. Cam was doing his best to keep it brief.

"No, I'm working," he said. "At the theater. Building props. Yeah, when I can. Have you eaten? Good."

"Yo Cam," I said. "Need you here."

"Gotta go," he said, and switched off, tucking the phone back into his pocket. I felt the light pressure of him painting the hinge on the other side.

"Everything ok?"

"Oh yeah. Suze was just checking in, wanted to know when I'd be home. Mom's out, Dad's at work, and she wants to take the dogs for a walk."

Suze was Cam's younger sister, now a freshman in high school. "It's good she does that," I said, and we continued on with our brushes.

An hour or so later, all our calm was shattered. Cam was working on the bottom set of hinges, and I was working on the top, keeping the screen balanced.

Cam's cell rang.

"*What?*" he exclaimed, his voice a horrified stage whisper. "What do you mean, they—"

My ears pricked up. They?

He saw me looking at him and turned away, although I could still hear him. "How? What do you mean, you think you forgot? Geez, Suze, Dad's gonna kill us! Do you know where—no, they wouldn't have just disappeared! Cripes!" He turned to me, blurted, "I have to go! Finish for us, ok?" and bounded off the stage, hurtling down an aisle as if the very Hounds of Hell were chasing him.

"Cam, what the—"

"The Bichons are loose!" He may as well have announced, "The Mongols are invading Poland!" and slammed out the doors to the sidewalk.

SIX

Tim and I got back to the shop around 8. The blocking was done, the furniture placement figured out, the players having practiced their choreography, and the hinges on the two screens were drying.

We hadn't heard anything from Cam yet.

Sometime around 9, we were just about ready to leave for the night, the closed sign having gone up hours ago. I was giving the counter one last swipe with a dustcloth, and Tim was bundling up the day's tallies and putting them in the safe when there was a knock at the door.

It was Sheriff Danielson, Steven to his friends or when he was off duty. I unlocked the door and promptly let him in, closing it behind him.

Tim closed the safe and joined us. "Hi," he said cheerfully. "Can we help you?"

Our Sheriff was a nice guy, very good at his job. We met him shortly after we opened. He'd come by to introduce himself and to give us his card. We showed him the shop and offered him a cup of espresso, and with that, a friendship bloomed. He was a little older than us, in his mid-30's if I had to guess.

"I wish I was here under better circumstances," he said now. "Johnny Martin's gone missing. His mom called a little bit ago. He's not here, is he?"

Tim and I looked at each other, shocked. We shook our heads.

"She can't find him anywhere. Do you recall her and Johnny coming here this afternoon?"

"Of course," I said, and related the details of their visit. "Johnny picked every single one of those books off the floor and stacked them up neatly for me. He's a good kid. He even apologized. Then they left. Once they were out the door, I went back to put the books away. I didn't even see them cross the street."

Steven nodded. "That was the last you saw of him?"

"Yes, sir."

"When did you leave the shop?"

"I was done by 5:30. Went over to Franco's and grabbed a bunch of pizzas for the cast and crew."

"What about you?" he asked Tim.

"I'd been in rehearsal with the rest of

the cast since about 4:30. Joc arrived around six, and everyone helped divest her of her burdens."

"And I happily took their money," I said.

We laughed, but it was strained.

"It's not just Johnny. Another boy's gone missing too. Mrs. Harris is very worried."

The other kid's name was Bobby Harris. Bobby was a happy, active kid about Johnny's age and also his best friend. He was fond of perusing the kids' section while his mother browsed.

Bobby had simply vanished. He was in their front yard playing with his catcher's mitt and baseball. When Ellen called him in a little later for supper, he simply wasn't there, but his gear was. She knew instantly that something was very wrong.

He always brought his stuff in.

Always.

The two boys were thought to have disappeared around the same time. It was assumed they were together because their routine in good weather was to go to the park.

Bobby's mom Ellen was a sweet woman who put in half-days as a postal worker while her son was in school. She was a gentle creature who wouldn't have hurt a tiger if it was charging straight at her. One time she was in the store when a rather large spider dropped from the ceiling and landed on her hand. She looked at it, laughed, and went outside to release it in the bushes. Unsurprisingly, she was a fan of cozy mysteries.

There was a Mr. Harris but I'd never met him. He drove for a long-haul trucking firm and was currently out of state.

What was left? Two ordinary families living two very ordinary sets of lives. No melodramas or phone calls or ransom notes.

None of their friends had seen them at the park. More than likely they'd just gotten distracted by something. The only logical conclusion was that the boys had wandered off and somehow managed to get themselves lost. Our little village was hidden by forest on two sides, one of them hugging a ridgeline. It made for lovely hiking, but if you didn't know the way, it was easy enough to get misplaced. We sometimes heard coyotes at night, but no one ever mentioned there being anything bigger or more dangerous than that. With a little luck, they'd be ok if they ended up bedding down for the night in the open on this balmy evening. Neither boy carried a cell phone.

"I guess that's all, then," Steven said.

"Let me know if you hear anything?"

"Absolutely," we said. "Good luck." For now, it was just the police department doing the search, as the area was rather limited. Like it or not, we still had a business to run so couldn't help and kept our ears to the ground.

SEVEN

Right after Steven left, the phone rang. Marion.

It was now ten o'clock. "Any news?" I asked.

"No." She sniffled, blew her nose. "Nothing on Bobby either."

"Is Rich there?"

At the sound of her husband's name, she started to cry. I heard a male voice in the background, heard someone taking the phone. "That you, Joc?"

"Yes Peter. Shall I come over?"

"The sooner the better," he said.

"On my way."

Peter opened the door. Marion was seated on the couch. I sat down next to her and put my arms around her, rocking her gently.

After a moment, she straightened. "I'm ok," she said, even though she clearly wasn't. "Rich isn't here. Business trip in Vegas. Peter came over to help."

I nodded. "So, what happened?"

"Johnny was running late, but that's understandable on a summer evening. I knew he'd be here soon enough. And then Ellen called me about Bobby, and we both started to get worried, and I called Sheriff Danielson. I figured Rich should know so I called him, but he kept ignoring me."

She hadn't gone all to pieces, not

even by the time she'd called Rich. Marion was a resourceful and practical soul, and it wasn't until Ellen had called her that she began to get worried and called Steven. She would have given Johnny until six, as that was their usual supper time. Steven assured her that they'd keep an eye for the boys, and he'd be in touch with both mothers. Two hours later, the kids had still not shown up, and that's when Marion started to get really worried.

The first thing she did was look up all the flights from Vegas to Portland for that night and into the very early morning. In the span of seven hours, Rich could have caught any one of the same number of planes and been back in his own living room in under four hours.

Then she called him. He didn't pick up. She tried several times and concluded that his phone had been turned off. She called the hotel, citing an emergency, and the staff confirmed he was out momentarily. Would she like them to contact her when he returned?

She would. This time Rich called her back, and he wasn't pleased. "And then Rich blew up all over me because he couldn't be bothered to answer his own damned phone." Her eyes were flashing, and she was starting to cry again. Peter handed her some more tissues.

"I told him that Johnny had gone missing and that no one could find him. I needed him to come home. Now. The next plane left in 45 minutes. He said kids went wandering off all the time, and when I said I knew something was wrong, he told me mother's intuition was for the birds and to quit overreacting.

"I wanted to yell at him, but it wouldn't have helped anything, so I asked him why he didn't answer his phone, and he gave me a line of crap about 'some very important business clients' and how he'd turned it off so he wouldn't be dragged into 'trite domestic matters.' He was angry at me, but I didn't care."

Rich's irritation was real, but Marion's was raw.

She'd exploded. She never bothered him on his business trips unless there was something very important going on. This was a crisis! His son could be in serious trouble. His wife was a mess and needed him. He needed to come home. Right now.

Rich finally relented a little. He said the kids were fine and just out exploring or something. They'd show up.

She did not agree. "I feel it, Rich. Something's wrong."

"He said, "You don't know what the hell you're talking about, Marion. I have to go.'"

And then his phone beeped. She'd stared at hers for a moment, stunned.

Had Rich just told her he was staying in Vegas?

"I couldn't believe it," Peter said. "His son is missing and whatever is going on in Vegas is more important?"

"He's probably partying it up pretending he's the man with the biggest dick," she said. "He told me he had some conferences with some 'important business contacts' and couldn't leave."

"Most of them with names like Tawny or Chantrelle or Jasmine," Peter snorted. "I'm sorry, Marion, that was uncalled for."

"Once Johnny comes home, I'm going to divorce that son of a bitch I was fool enough to marry," Marion said coldly. "It's over."

EIGHT

Sometime around noon on Day Two, Rich finally showed up. Johnny and Bobby were still missing. Rich was pissed that he'd had to call a cab from the airport because his wife was too busy with some wild goose chase regarding his kid who was probably going to stroll in the door any minute. Rich walked into his living room only to be met by her and the Sheriff for some ridiculous questioning. He didn't have Johnny packed in his suitcase now, did he?

Steven was convinced of the veracity

of his story, as far as it went. Yes, he was in Vegas on a business trip, and no, he'd gotten away as quickly as he could. Steven and Marion were both convinced that on the latter point it was due to some distraction or other, none of which had anything to do with Johnny who'd probably ended up at a sleepover and forgotten to tell his mom.

"No red-eye flights?" Steven had asked. "Couldn't get an emergency flight?"

"No luck," Rich said. "They told me they were swamped with conventioneers on top of the usual tourists. Hundreds of them. No flights available. Best I could get wasn't until this morning. I took it."

All easy enough to check. Steven thanked him for his time and left.

Marion was having none of it. If it had been her, she'd have come home in the frigging wheel well if she had to. He thought she was being ridiculous and making a great fuss over nothing. She knew she wasn't.

Rich brought his suitcase upstairs and dumped it on their bed, headed for the shower. Marion pulled his dirty clothes out. She sniffed. Held up a shirt and sniffed again.

As she thought. His trips away allowed him to leave his wife with all the work and responsibility while he hotly pursued his midlife crisis. Sleepovers, indeed.

God only knew what else he brought home. She resolved to see a doctor for a checkup in the next week or so.

Rich emerged from the shower. She'd shoved the shirt under his nose. "Does this smell like Opium to you? Because it does to me."

Marion wore tea rose, not musk.

He'd wrenched away from her. "Oh,

come on! It's just hotel laundry soap!" The fact that he couldn't look at her gave him away.

"Anything else you'd like to tell me, other than that you're sleeping on the couch?"

"That's not fair! I just got home from an exhausting tri—"

She'd snorted. "I'll bet it was exhausting."

"Would you sto—"

"Shut up, Rich. Find our child." The anger would keep her going, see her through this even as her heart broke. It had to. "It will," she assured me. "It will."

I was not so certain.

Ellen had gotten in touch with her husband within hours of the disappearance. Max Harris was somewhere three states away when Bobby had vanished, so was immediately removed from the suspect list. He headed home as soon as he'd been able to get his haul offloaded to another trucker with his company, and his boss bought him a round-trip ticket and shoved him on a plane. His flight from Arizona had a brief stopover in Las Vegas, and he still beat Rich Martin home by a good three hours.

NINE

The mail arrived, dropping through the wall slot to the basket below. I picked it up and set it on the counter. Amid the usual bills, catalogs, and junk mail was a small plain white envelope, addressed simply to "Lock & Key." Intrigued, I opened that first. A neatly trimmed photo, probably done on a home printer using regular office paper, emerged. There was something written underneath it. The photo was interesting—it was a black and white ground level view of what appeared to be an opening or void in the street. Very film noir, and quite evocative. I pulled it out all the way and frowned.

Tim said, "You've got that look, Joc."

No surprises there. Tim said "that look" was my tell, and why I was such an awful poker player.

"Yeah," I said, turning the paper over and seeing nothing. "Huh."

"No signature?"

"Not that I can see."

"What does it say?"

"'Worn with walking, Marco stands nameless'," I read aloud. "Marco?"

"Polo," Tim replied automatically, taking it from me.

"Shit," I said.

He raised an eyebrow. He knew where my mind had wandered.

It went to things which were lost.

Naturally, we called Steven right away. He came right down and examined the note thoroughly. The handwriting was fairly nondescript, just an average cursive hand penning a cryptic note. "So what tipped you off?" he asked.

"The game," I said. "Marco!"

"Polo!" Tim replied automatically.

"See?"

"So who's trying to find what?" Steven asked. "Or who?"

"We were hoping you'd know," Tim said. "The kids are still missing, aren't they?"

"This doesn't sound like a ransom note or anything like that," Steven said.

"No," I agreed. "It sounds...tired. A little confused."

"I don't know, guys," he said. "I have no idea what to make of it. But it is intriguing. Mind if I keep this for now?"

"Please do."

"Do you think they slept somewhere?" Tim asked.

"Somewhere. I'm thinking they might have gotten lost in the woods. Thank God it's summer." He looked out the window, then at us. "We'll find them. Anything, ok?"

"Of course."

"Thank you." He looked at the photo again. "It's probably nothing, but you never know." He tucked it back in its envelope and slipped it into his breast pocket. The door jangled.

At the Martin's, Rich finally admitted to himself that his wife just might be onto something and took them both to the police station. The officer on duty brought them coffee, allowed them to stay for an hour, and gently suggested that they go home, that they'd be the first to know. With nothing else to do, they got back in the car and went.

At Ellen's, Max Harris and his wife comforted each other, their phones never more than a few inches away.

The peripheral dramas played out. The day turned to twilight, and the dusk morphed into another long and restless night.

TEN

Day Three. There was still no sign of the kids.

We were just about to open for the day. Tim was in the storage nook pulling some overstock when he heard odd scrabbling beneath the floorboards. Emerging from behind the curtain with a pile of books, he said, "Time to call the exterminator."

Nuts, I thought. "So soon? They were just here a few weeks ago." High summer, cool, dark places, and vermin just went together. To date, they hadn't entered the shop, and we didn't want them to.

I got on the cell and called X-Pest, our local go-to company, and got their receptionist right away. "Hi Carrie. This is Joc at Lock & Key. We seem to have a critter problem under the floor."

She moaned.

"Are you ok?" I asked.

She sighed. "Hon, you're the fourth call I've had this morning about the same problem. It's weird. Days apart is normal, but within a few hours?"

"Wow," I said. "So, what's going on?"

She sounded exasperated. "Either the vermin have had a population explosion, or they called in their buddies and are taking over the town. The phone started ringing at six, and we don't even open until eight. All on the other side of the park from you."

"Well, they've hit us now," I said.

I heard one of the extensions ring. "Hang on, I'll be right back." She punched "hold," and I looked through the titles Tim had brought to the counter.

Carrie came back on. "Hon, that was Mick. He says he and Aaron are going down into the underground tunnels to see if that's the source of the problem. They're going to check the east side first, starting with the water pipes, then come over to your end."

"Sounds good." Aaron was the town inspector, a thorough and conscientious soul. He took great pride in keeping our little jewel of a town in perfect working order, and always kept his HazMat suit at the ready.

Tim motioned for the phone. "Hi, Carrie? This is Tim. Yes, under the storeroom. Yes, just scrabbling. It seems to have stopped for now. Thanks so much, we'll be here."

He hung up. "Sometime this afternoon, she thinks. Depends what they find."

"What about the noises?" I asked.

"Same noise. Everyone's hearing the same sounds."

It was eleven o'clock when I returned from the deli down the street with our lunch orders. Cobb salad, pure heaven on a hot day.

Tim was nowhere to be seen. As I put our salads in the little fridge, I noticed that fresh coffee was brewing. Sumatran with vanilla bean. Lovely stuff.

I went back out on the floor. There were no customers that I could see. "Tim?" I called. "You there?"

I heard a muffled voice. "Joc? Need you—bring a flashlight!"

"Where are you?" I asked, dredging in our toolbox for one and checking to see that it worked.

"Storeroom! There's something else here, something we missed! Close us down for 10 minutes, will you?"

"Yup," I said, pulling out the clock sign and setting the arms. After hanging it up and locking the door, I hurried to join my partner.

He'd been busy in my absence. All of the backstock and shelving had been removed and were sitting in tidy stacks outside the entry.

I crawled in and found Tim inside on his hands and knees, feeling the joins of the walls and floor, tapping on both, listening.

"What are you looking for?" I asked.

"I bumped into a narrow ridge in the wall when I was pulling stock just now," he said. He rose and moved up the far wall, felt something. "There you are, you little bugger!"

I turned the flashlight beam on his find.

There was some kind of a doorway-shaped seam on one of the walls. It had been sealed and painted over, but nonetheless, it was there, something we'd passed a thousand times and never noticed.

I fished in my pocket for a pencil, handed it to him. He carefully drew the outline, tapping and feeling, following the subtle changes of sound and texture. I kept my light on him.

He was three-quarters of the way done when I stopped him. "I want to see something," I said. I turned off the flashlight.

Our eyes adjusted. We looked at the wall, blinking, and realized why we'd never seen this before.

The wall showed no signs of any latches, hinges, or closures of any sort. That meant that possibly these features were on the other side or had been removed before the doorway was sealed. Something had been placed between the gaps of the door and the wall, then sealed, smoothed over, and painted to match the interior wall. There was just enough of a texture difference for it to be noticeable by touch, but it was all but invisible to the naked eye.

And we noticed something else.

Noises, faint still, on the other side. They stopped.

An impulse seized me. A picture depicting a paused journey.

"MARCO!" I shouted, louder than I'd ever shouted before.

A mad scrabbling, high pitched barking. I'd know K2's voice anywhere!

"MARCO!" Tim joined me, his stage-trained voice resonating magnificently through the walls.

We heard feet—small human feet—rushing toward us. 'POLO!!! POLO!" Frantic young voices, full of hope.

"Johnny, Bobby—stay right where you are. You're on the other side of the bookstore. This is Tim. Joc is on the phone getting help. Are you guys ok?"

"We got lost," Johnny said.

"There was a hole and then it wasn't there anymore and—" The voice dissolved into snuffles.

"Everything's ok now, boys. We just need to get some help to break down the wall. Stick with me, ok?"

"I want my mom," Johnny said.

"Me too!" Bobby agreed.

"You two will be the most wonderful things they will ever see in their whole lives," Tim said. "They'll be here soon."

I stepped into the store proper and

pulled out my cell, called Steven.

"Hi Joc. What's—"

"We found them," I said in a rush. "They're alive. They sound ok, but we can't get to them, we need a sledgehammer, and oh my God, their parents and—"

"Call them," he said. "We're on our way."

I did. Both sets of parents were enroute.

Called Cam. "They're here and are all right," I said, and the disconnection was done before I'd even finished the sentence.

I reached across the countertop, grabbing a tissue to catch the tears of relief. Wiping my eyes, I flipped our door sign to "Closed for the day. We're sorry we missed you!"

ELEVEN

Two days after the boys were found, the anonymous note somehow made the weekly paper.

No one was more surprised than the two of us and Steven. We were the only ones who even knew it existed beyond the person who made it. It was likely to assume that the maker thought the photo had never left the shop once it had been delivered to us. The manhole cover was no big deal, assuming anyone had noticed it at all.

We had no way of knowing that

some blocks away, Ellie Lewis all but froze with shock when she opened the morning paper to see the photo and the caption in huge black ink: "WAS THIS A CLUE???"

Cam came into the kitchen just in time to see his mother faint.

She came to lying on the couch with Cam holding a cup of warm tea for her. "Drink this, Mom," he said kindly.

She did. "Cam...the...the paper...."

"I'll get it. You sit up slowly and drink your tea." When he rejoined her, he asked, "What's this got to do with you?"

She told him about the picture as far as she knew it. "It was a story idea—I wanted to run it past Tim and Joc. But how on earth did it get in the paper? Tim and Joc wouldn't have done it, for sure, and no one else knew about it. This makes no sense." She shook her head. "It was just a story idea. I didn't even sign it.

That's all. Now I'm afraid to do anything with it."

"I think you should do what you want, Mom. Give it a shot."

"Thank you, honey." She sipped. "Well, I was kind of shy and feeling a bit silly, so I just dropped it in their box. The plan was to talk with them later. But then this whole thing with the boys happened, and then they were found, and my photo was so close to what happened to them and I can understand Tim and Joc being puzzled under the circumstances and maybe passing it along to Sheriff Daniels, but when I'd left it there absolutely no one except the boys knew where they were, and...oh, hell!" She plucked a tissue from the box on the coffee table and blew her nose. "And now I should talk with them and Sheriff Daniels and fess up to it because the rumor mill's going to be all over it, and we all know

70

what a mess that can be."

"Mom, you didn't do anything," Cam said.

"But I did. By omission. I want to know what the missing parts are. I want the whole thing to be published in the paper so everyone realizes just how bad bad timing can be and how it's good to get the truth out quickly so no more harm is done. Will you come with me?"

"Sure," he said. He kissed her on the cheek. "I'm really proud of you, Mom."

Late afternoon on the day that the boys disappeared, Ellie was driving down the street that went past the park and noticed that a manhole cover was askew. She figured some city worker was down under the street and never gave it another thought. But in the moment of seeing the manhole cover lying tip tilted, she was inspired by the overall visual effect of sun and shadow on the pavement and stopped to take a picture of it. We didn't know she was working on something and had dropped us a teaser.

What we saw, true to form for mystery lovers everywhere, was a clue.

It wasn't until the next day that Ellie heard about the boys.

Ellie wasn't the only one to see the paper that morning. There was some heated discussion between the city worker and his boss too. The worker had dragged the manhole cover partway off when dispatch called him away. Figuring that the gap between the cover and the hole wasn't big enough to be a problem, he left it, promising himself to come back later. Unfortunately, he ended up getting delayed for a few hours, and by the time he returned to it, he was in a hurry and neglected to go into the hole to see if anyone was down there. Instead, he called down a perfunctory "Hello! Anyone there?" and upon hearing nothing, pulled the cover back into place.

And that's exactly what he told his boss.

Later in the day, they both made their sincerest apologies to the public, the boss stressing due diligence and safety protocols and how this sort of thing would never happen again.

TWELVE

A week later all the dust had settled, and our little patch of paradise was back to being its lovely cordial self. Ellie was never in trouble and everyone pretty much sided with her. Sometimes bad things just happen, was the general accord. How was she to know?

Ellie invited the boys, their moms, and Tim and I over to tell their stories. We were open that day. Tim said he owed me for all the time I'd covered for him.

Over iced tea and fruit popsicles,

under a shade tree on a warm summer day, the atmosphere could not have been more serene for the telling of harrowing stories. Everyone shared their adventures, and the afternoon ended with hugs and an invitation to come by any time. A gracious and thoughtful hostess, Ellie listened carefully, catching every nuance.

The boys had quite a tale to tell. They were very brave in the face of what must have been a terrifying experience.

Johnny started it off, revealing that his mom had packed him two peanut butter sandwiches and a bottle of water, something she often did after soccer practice. It was just after four, and dinner was still hours away.

On the way to the park, he saw Bobby in his front yard, tossing a baseball up into the air and catching it in his mitt. He asked Bobby if he wanted to come and play in the park. Bobby did and stuck his nose in the door to tell his mom, but she had the mixer going and didn't hear him. "Come on!" Johnny had said, so Bobby left his things tucked by a bush, figuring he'd put them away when he got back.

The two boys crossed the empty street and went down the sidewalk to the park. Johnny was flipping a quarter when he lost control of it, and it fell with a distinctive clink and clatter. They watched the quarter bounce and fall into a hole next to a manhole cover.

This put a whole new spin on things. They went to the opening and looked in. Something was glimmering a few feet down. The next thing they knew, they had squeezed past the manhole cover and jumped into some kind of hole. Bobby saw the quarter and gave it back.

Looking around, they realized they

were in a kind of tunnel. "This is so cool!" Bobby said, and they decided to go exploring, using only the dim light from the overheads. The street noises above them became fierce creatures in the African bush, and the tunnel offshoots were great places to hide.

The boys realized some time later that they were in trouble. They'd managed to get lost, but being brave explorers and having seen enough cable shows where survival was predicated on the thoughtful use of resources, they decided to play it smart and ration their as yet untouched supplies. Each took two bites of sandwich and a swallow of water, and they found themselves walking where it was very quiet, not knowing how late it was and that the park was above them. Eventually they found a corner to sleep in. The tunnels were quite dry, cool but not cold.

They had no idea how far they'd gone.

They were afraid and all alone. Being brave, they decided to continue being brave and try to sleep.

Until they heard the scrabbling on the floor. They sat up, only to find themselves being viciously licked to death.

The Bichons had escaped a prison of their own, according to what Suze had told Cam. She'd taken them for a walk, come home, and thought she had closed the gate behind her, but the dogs had other ideas and noticed once she'd gone in that it wasn't secure. Off they went to invade Poland or the park, whichever was closer.

As near as anyone could figure, they went down the rabbit hole and sometime after that the manhole cover was put back.

The boys shared a sandwich with the dogs, much to their mutual delight, and they all curled up to sleep.

On the third morning, Carrie started getting phone calls. By the time Mick and Aaron showed up, the foursome was long gone. The dogs had gotten their bearings and were on their way home.

"Quite the adventure," I said.

"Let's just not repeat it, ok?" Marion said.

Everyone assented and rose. "We should do this again," Ellie said, and everyone agreed.

As I left, Ellie gently took my arm. "Research," she said softly, and winked.

She was writing again.

THIRTEEN

Marion and Johnny stopped by the shop. Johnny asked me for a few minutes of my time while Marion hit the stacks.

He wanted to know about mysteries for kids his age. He may have been ten, but he read at college level, and he reasoned things out in ways kids his age might otherwise not. I suspect he got his smarts from his mother.

"I'm delighted you're taking an interest in them," I said as we went to the Young Sleuths section. "You didn't used to be."

"Yeah," he said.

Something was clearly bothering him. "What's up?"

"About the photo...it still bugs me. I mean, I know what happened and that the whole thing was coincidental, but I heard it wasn't."

Oh crap. The gossip squad no doubt, led by a certain Mrs. Elizabeth Holbrook. "Who told you that?"

"Mrs. Holbrooke. She said Mrs. Lewis knew we were down there and left us there on purpose."

Why was I not surprised? "For starters, Mrs. Lewis emphatically did not know anyone was down there. She took the picture because it was interesting and shared it with us anonymously because she was running a story idea in her head and didn't want to give it away. We thought the photo was interesting too, and shared some thoughts on it with

Sheriff Daniels, who asked if he could borrow it. Someone stole it off his desk and gave it to the paper. Mrs. Lewis didn't know any of that until the paper came. So no, Mrs. Lewis had nothing to do with any of it. You haven't asked her about it, have you, beyond our visit?"

"No," he said, his eyes troubled. "I didn't want to upset her."

"And you know perfectly well Mrs. Lewis would have been the first to get help," I said, a bit sternly.

"I know," he said, looking at the floor.

"That was very kind of you not to speak to Mrs. Lewis about this, Johnny. It would have been very painful for her if you had."

"What about Mrs. Holbrooke?"

"Mrs. Holbrooke is a gossip. She and her friends like to spread stories around, whether they're true or not. Ignore them. Be polite, but otherwise don't listen to them. People like that can cause a lot of hurt and damage to other people."

Nearby, I saw Marion give me a thumbs-up.

He nodded. "So...are they lying?"

"In a way," I said. "They're telling the story the way they want it, because it's more exciting for them that way. There's usually some truth, but how much depends on them."

"That's really mean," he said.

"Yes, it is, and it can cause a lot of problems. That's why it's best not to pay them any attention. That way you don't give them a chance to make a story even worse."

"They should go climb trees or something."

I couldn't help grinning. "Can you imagine them up there, waving their foofy hats and yelling for help getting down?"

We broke out in giggles.

"Ah, here we go," I said, pulling out a title. "It's written for teenagers, but I think you will enjoy it." As a bookseller, our conversation told me a lot about him. This kid would be bored to death with books written for ten-year-olds.

He took it. "Ms. Joc? How do you know if you're going to like a book?"

"I usually read the front and back covers to see if it sounds interesting, then read the first ten pages. If I'm still interested, it comes home with me."

That made sense. "Do you have a lot of books?"

"Oh my, yes. Floor to ceiling. Somewhere in there, I have actual furniture." I winked.

He laughed. "Why is there a number 1 on the cover?"

"It's the first of a series—there are nine to date, and there's another on the way by the end of the year."

"If I like this book, should I get them all today?"

Marion was an aisle over. I could swear I saw her ears reaching our way.

"No," I laughed. "If you like this one, why don't you get the first two and go from there? Tell your mom and she can tell me. I'll pull them for you and make sure you get them."

Another thumbs-up from Marion.

Johnny lit up like a Christmas tree. "That would be awesome!"

An hour later, they were done, and I bagged their titles separately—Marion's usual pile and now Johnny's two. He was grinning from ear to ear. "I can hardly wait!" he exclaimed.

"We hope you enjoy them," I said, slipping two of our fancy store bookmarks into their bags to mark this auspicious day.

As Johnny had made clear, not everyone was so willing to set the episode in the history books and move on. Not by a long shot.

FOURTEEN

It's amazing what you can find at a grocery store.

"Well, if it hadn't been for Georgia here, we would never have known about it at all, would we, Georgia?"

I'd have known that simpering voice anywhere. Mrs. Elizabeth Holbrook. She was a good client—and one of the nastiest-minded women I'd ever met. She wore a mid-calf lilac silk summer dress and a summer hat that was swathed in sheer white silk and tiny lavender flowers. She looked for all the world like a perfect lady, sophisticated, attractive, and was, right until she opened her mouth. The phrase "crushing the serpent's head" came unbidden to my mind. She might have been decorative, but she needed someone to drop a rock on her.

A big, heavy rock.

Everyone except her besties called her "Mrs. Holbrook." It wasn't meant to be complimentary, but she was oblivious to that. To her friends, she was a very dignified "Elizabeth."

She and her bevy were standing just outside the door to the grocery store, all but blocking traffic in either direction. Carrying two full shopping totes, I stopped short and cleared my throat loudly. "Excuse me, ladies!"

"Oh dear!" someone exclaimed, and the whole lot of them pattered out of the way. "Thank you," I said, and had one of those flashes when you just know you need to set those heavy bags down and rest a moment. I walked to the nearest big brick planter box, sat on the edge, put my bags down on the walk, and pretended to be going through them looking for something.

The women completely ignored me.

Another woman spoke—Georgia, I assumed. "Oh please. I was putting his mail down and noticed it just lying there with a sticky note on it."

"Ooo, what did it say?" someone asked.

"It just had one word on it." She paused for effect. "'Clue?'"

Mrs. Holbrooke said, "Now Georgia, don't be a tease."

"I'm not," she said. "That was the word, followed by a question mark. You can imagine what I thought! Well, I had to see more, so I checked to make sure no one was around, and when I went back to look at it, I heard him coming, so I quickly slipped it into my shift pocket, putting his mail down on the spot."

"Clever Georgia!" someone said.

"I got to the door just in time for him to hold it open for me."

Everyone laughed.

"And of course, I took it to the paper after seeing what it was, on the grounds they copy and give it back right away so I could return it."

"How handy to be a volunteer at the Village office," Mrs. Holbrooke said. Again, giggles. "Of course, that little fool Ellie—can you imagine her going to the police with that wild story?"

"The Sheriff probably thought it was ridiculous," one of the women sniffed, and everyone nodded in agreement.

"No doubt," her lead detractor said. "Just some wild fantasy from some lunatic housewife."

That's when I saw Cam coming on full intercept. Armed with the Bichons and pure fury. "Hey, Mrs. Holbrook!" he yelled.

She swiveled to look at him. Her lips curled in distaste at the dogs. Probably because a low rumble was issuing from around Cam's ankles. "Oh, for heaven's sake, Cam, do take those horrid creatures somewhere else. Vicious little rats!"

K2 and Matt took umbrage at this and growled even louder, not that I blame them. They had their hackles up, tails down and ears back. Cam raised a hand. "I got this, guys," he said, and they quieted.

"Really?" he asked. "Really? Are you kidding me? You lie about my mother, who's one of the bravest people I've ever met, and you insult my dogs, who have much better manners than you do. Who do you think you're kidding?"

Go Cam! I cheered in my head.

Not about to be dethroned by the teenage son of her latest prey, she turned on her sweetest, most sympathetic voice. "Now Cam, I don't blame you," she cooed. "She *is* your mother, after all. Of *course* you want to protect her."

"Shut up!" Cam shouted, loud enough for the entire parking lot to hear. "You nasty lying bitch! Shut up!"

"Cam!" she gasped dramatically, putting a hand to her bosom in shock. "How *dare* you spea—"

"Hey Cam!" I called, thinking it was about time to defuse this confrontation.

He'd been getting ready to say something else, heard me, and looked at me like he was seeing me for the first time.

"I saw your mom a little bit ago—she

92

said you're out of milk. Do you need any money?"

Cam caught up fast. "Yeah, that's why I'm here." He pulled out his wallet. "Nope, all good. Could you watch the dogs?"

"Get out of here," I said teasingly, tossing my head toward the doors. Grinning, he released their leashes and they happily piled into me. "Is you fierce guard dogs?" I baby-talked them. "Yes you is. The fiercest *ever*..."

Mrs. Elizabeth Holbrook gave me a look that could have turned rosewater to arsenic. I pretended to ignore her, playing with the pups. Her audience, seeing that today's installment of "Town Gossip" was over, dispersed. She tipped her head up in contempt and strutted back to her car, shutting the door behind her. A bit over firmly, I thought.

I heard later that Georgia came

home to a big surprise—a certain sheriff, one officer, and a search warrant.

I went shopping the day after Georgia got served, telling myself I was going because I needed carrots, not because I was going to spy. The gaggle tended to gather at the same time, more or less, and I just happened to luck into them. Of course I did.

Sure enough, I walked out of the grocery with my bag of carrots and sundries and sat on the planter box pretending to scrutinize my receipt when I heard Georgia's breathless voice.

"Oh, my dears, I thought I was going to faint! That officer had a gun trained on me, and the Sheriff ordered me to let them in, shoving a piece of paper in my face!"

"He *what*?" asked someone in a horrified voice.

"What kind of paper?" Mrs. Holcombe asked breathlessly, eager for more.

"A *gun*?"

Georgia's tone turned to one of indignation. "I'm hardly afraid of guns, Louisa," she snapped. "It was a search warrant, if you must know. The nerve!" She paused a moment. "And then they came in, and that Sheriff said he would spare me the indignity of searching my house if I answered one question truthfully—when have I ever lied?"

Much denial from the gaggle.

"Well, of course I told him that, and he could put that gun down before I told him anything. Imagine pulling a gun on a lady!"

"Yes Georgia, we know all that. So, what happened?"

"Well, he asked me if there was anything from his office in my house, and I said no, why would there be, and he told me about that picture having gone missing—of course I'd returned it as soon as I could! I couldn't have been gone more than an hour or so! But he permanently banned me from the police department! He said I was the only one who could have taken it, but of course I didn't tell him that. The nerve!"

I left, unnoticed amidst all the patting and sympathizing. Once home, I called Steven and told him the latest. The story was so ridiculous we were both dying with laughter.

"By the way Steven, what was your man holding that she thought was a gun?"

"A clipboard," he said, sighing. "Oh well, better nip this one in the bud. Thanks, Joc."

FIFTEEN

A few days later, I took a moment before we opened for a sip of espresso and a scan through the village paper.

"Tim!" I called. "Stuff whatever you're doing in the safe and come here!"

Tim did our daily tallies every morning and handled whatever paperwork needed to be handled that day. I heard our safe squeak closed. We never oiled it—the sound was so distinctive and loud that we would have known in an instant if someone other than us opened it.

Coffee cup in hand, he came to the counter. "What's up?

"Listen to this," I said, holding the paper up. "On the Editorials page, no less."

There is in our quiet town a Medusa. It spreads untruths about people, its many heads poking into places where it has no right to go. It picks at the edges of peoples' lives and creates anger and misunderstanding. It doesn't seek the truth; it only believes in its own version, reeking of falsehood. Arguing with it only feeds it, as it turns your words against you. It is a liar, and like all liars, it seeks all of the glory and doesn't care what— or who—it destroys.

Its name is Gossip, and it needs to be shut down.

The events of the last month or so have put all of us on shaky ground, some more than others. For those most directly involved, they need time to heal, not have their lives disrupted even more by someone else's evil words.

We are a community of good people. Let's stand strong and be honest with each other. Our respect for ourselves alone deserves nothing less.

"'Most sincerely, Mrs. Ellie Lewis'"

"Wow!" Tim exclaimed. "Go get 'em, Ellie!"

"I know, right? And she never mentioned even one name, not one. No one can come after her about it." Mrs. Holbrook was probably spitting nails!

That afternoon, Cam stopped by for a moment with a message from his mom. We'd sent her a gift of a potted purple chrysanthemums, a flower she loved, with a note enclosed:

"GREAT editorial! You have so got this!" An initialed smiley emoticon from each of us.

Cam said he hadn't seen his mother look that happy in a long time. "She's signed up to take some college writing classes in the fall."

"That's great!" we exclaimed.

"And Dad's supporting her, too!" he enthused.

"She's on a roll," Tim said.

"Tell her we're counting on hosting her book signing," I said, grinning.

"Oh, I will!"

And I hope with all my heart that Ellie reserves a special spot in her books for the Mrs. Holbrooks of this world.

SIXTEEN

As they say, the show must go on. And so it did, once the boys were back in town rather than under it.

Princes In The Tower was a play about office politics and demagoguery, of how the ego of one can denigrate and ruin the lives of many while it destroys itself. As any critic might say, it was interesting and relevant. And now that the sets were done, rehearsals could begin in earnest. We were opening the last weekend of July, with additional performances the first weekend of

August. Perfect for getting folks between summer vacations, with no worries about conflicting with any early starts on school activities or Labor Day.

At the moment, it was the opening of Act I, scene 1. Tim 's character entered stage right, looking up at a clock hanging on the office wall. "The day begins," he said to himself, and continued across, exiting stage left. He returned and took center stage, a coffee mug in hand. "She expects her coffee on her desk at nine sharp," he said, bustling offstage again. His role was similar to that of the Stage Manager in *Our Town*—he was the guiding force behind the action, the omniscient observer and commentator masquerading as a personal secretary. A few seconds later, a woman followed him, stopping where he had stopped, but instead of looking at the clock, she turned outwards toward the seats to address her world.

Susan Jarrett was playing the female lead. She was a short little dumpling of a woman, so contrary in appearance to her role. The look on her face clearly stated that she thought she was batty for trying this. Her acting experience was limited to high school, she'd said, yet she found community theater in her 30's and was welcomed into the fold, much to her shock. Even more to her surprise, she was quite good.

Our director, Peter Fokes, sat offside, script in lap, watching her. He nodded at her. "And...go."

Now she was looking out at all the empty seats, and stage fright caught her. Making a conscious effort to pull herself together, she began her opening soliloquy. "I am queen," she said in a timorous voice. She stopped. "Well, that stank."

"It did indeed," Peter said. "And now that you have it out of your system, it's time to own it."

"Peter, this character is such a first-class bitch she deserves to be horsewhipped."

"Of course she does. What's her main personality attribute?"

"She believes in eating people she thinks are competing with her for breakfast. And she's paranoid enough to think everyone is competing with her."

"There you go."

They continued chatting about realizing the Bitch Queen for a few more minutes. As they talked, I remembered something and went into the prop room, where I shared duties with Marion. After digging through a few boxes, I found my prize. I brought it out to Susan, the object held carefully in both hands, bowed to her, and settled a very royal (if somewhat worn) looking tiara on her head, bowing and stepping back.

Peter smiled. He gave her the thumbs-up.

Susan took one step forward, one hand brushing her imaginary skirts behind her. "I am Queen," she proclaimed, her voice giving no room for quarter or dispute. "*I* am. They call me a Junior Exec, but it is *my* word which moves this place or brings it to a screeching halt. The suits can say whatever they want, locked up in their offices with their 'very important work' and their client Jack Daniels. Not one of them knows what goes on around here, and they won't." She laughed harshly, then mocked, "'Ms. Dover, the CEO wants to know what we did with that account.'" She parroted his voice. "'I did what you told me to, sir', I'll say sweetly, and they leave here confused and frantic because they can't remember what they told me and think that I've moved on and forgotten all about it. Like hell I forgot. Poor little suits, their seams are ripping. And everyone here knows it. RAY! Is that my coffee?"

She stopped and broke character. "How was that?"

"Great," Peter said, and meant it. "Remind me never to work for you. Seriously Susan. Just what I was looking for."

She looked over at me. I gave her two thumbs up. "I think someone gave me a magic hat," she said, grinning. "I'd like to keep using on it."

Corrine, our amazing costumer, stepped in and removed it from her head. "It's had a run," she said, examining it inside and out. The band was stained and more than a bit tatty. Rhinestones of various sizes were missing from sundry places, including the capstone which had been, presumably, the most spectacular of them all. "How about I see if I can find its twin and we use both in the show?"

I could see Peter's brain mulling this over, running through the acts in his head, deciding where and when each tiara might be appropriate. "It's a grand idea," he said. "This would be perfect for the final scene just as it is, maybe even a little more so. But we don't want to damage it."

"I can add smudges and marks to it which will come out easily," Corrine said. "It will be fine. And the new one could be used for the rest of her scenes."

"What if you can't find one?" he asked.

"Then I'll make one."

"That's a lot of work. And a lot of rhinestones."

They all turned and looked at Tim, who had silently come up and joined us. He always said that if you can't move quietly on stage, you have no business being there. Of course, no one ever heard him coming.

Corrine smiled.

Susan giggled. "She has a rhinestone collection to rival the gold in Fort Knox," she said. "It's mind boggling."

"Let's see how this looks," Peter suggested. "Final scene."

Tim took his spot center stage. Corrine took the tiara and moved to the side, kneeling on the floor with the tiara on its side under one hand ready to go.

Peter said, "The lights are coming down. It's getting darker and darker. In the background, Ms. Dover staggers about the office, bumping into overturned furniture, crying out from time to time when she hits something, her voice gradually fading off. The noise of movement stops. Only one light remains, falling on her assistant. He stands there listening as the cries die out. A battered tiara rolls—Corrine!—toward him and wobbles to a halt at his feet. Kneeling, he picks it up..."

Tim knelt, and reverently lifted it in both hands.

"The crown is broken off in spots, scorched and battered. Ms. Dover is silent and unseen."

Tim slowly spun around, offering the tiara to the office workers. There were no takers—everyone had long since fled. He faced the audience again.

"All is ruin," he said, his cadence pitched in a minor key, off just enough to induce a major creep factor. His voice floated like a spirit to the back of the theater, filling every crevice. He set the tiara on the floor and stepped back into the darkness.

"The spotlight holds the tiara for a moment, gradually going black. Curtain."

I shivered.

Everyone looked at me and nodded.

"This is going to be great," Peter said.

No one disagreed with him.

We picked up again in the middle of Act I. Mr. Rice, antagonist to Ms. Dover and played convincingly by Ed Graham, made his way in, brushing his way past her secretary in a burst of male authority and superiority. Ray grabbed some papers and got to her first, all but slamming the door in his face. "She can't see you now," he said.

"Hey!"

"What is it, Ray?" she asked,

annoyed.

"Mr. Rice—"

She looked skyward in exasperation.

"He's sent these papers over for you to sign." He moved to lay them on her desk, but she snatched them from his hand and took out a red marker. "Sit," she ordered, and he did, in one of the low chairs kept for visitors.

"No, no, no—who the hell does he think he's kidding? Five mill for that acquisition? It's barely worth two hundred k, and that's on a good day...." She finished her notes, put the pen back in her desk drawer. "All right. You can let him in now."

Rice entered, all slickness and snake oil. Glaring at Ray, he said, "Ah, I see you have my papers. I trust we have an agreement."

She'd risen, papers in hand. "We most emphatically do not. You know perfectly well the property's not worth even half that. Try again, buster." She handed him the papers, and tried to stare him down, the voltage of the malevolence high between them. Two alpha dogs, neither about to give in.

They froze in place.

"Lights fade on Rice and Dover, come up on Ray. Soliloquy."

Tim rose, stepped to the side, and gestured to the shadows. "There they are frozen, the princes in the tower. The walls which enclose them blind them to the folly of sovereignty. Beyond them, it all means nothing, this land of sales and acquisitions and who is the best dealer of the poker game. There are no jackpots. Only egos twisting in the wind. The structure will fall, and others tread unwittingly across their ashes."

SEVENTEEN

I decided it was time to make an embroidery piece for the shop, one that spoke to our theme, and that would, of course, hang over our mantelpiece. Figuring out what to do was tough enough—mysteries are full of murder and mayhem, neither of which were conducive to a cozy bookshop that welcomes children. Nor did I want to do portraits of famous sleuths—Holmes, Poirot, and their ilk—or their creators. I didn't want a piece that would look like a game of Clue. Colonel Mustard would just have to go on hold for a while.

I finally chose to do a parlor, similar to our own at Lock & Key. The final sketch showed a fireplace with a cozy fire burning, a small table nearby holding a Victorian lamp, and a crystal brandy snifter with just the right amount of the amber fluid. Next to it, a large, overstuffed armchair sat facing three-quarters out toward the viewer, a slightly wrinkled antimacassar draped across the back. An open book spraddled across one of the arms, the title on the spine just hinted at. A pair of wire-rimmed spectacles sat half open on the seat cushion. Where could the reader have gone?

When I showed my finished sketches to Tim, he grinned like a schoolboy. "What a neat illusion," he said. "Almost surreal. It's going to blow their minds, Joc."

I blew on my fingernails and buffed them on my shirt. "Yeah?"

"Yeah. The lady has the mad skills, she does. How big is it going to be?"

We continued to discuss the project, my little needleworker's heart skipping with delight.

One gorgeous evening after closing, I wanted to spend some time on the store needlework project in the fresh air. Tim was at rehearsal, and my services weren't needed. Gathering my needles and threads, breaking down my embroidery stand and throwing everything into my craft bag, I headed out the door and walked down to the park. I found an empty bench under a lovely shade tree and was happily stitching away when I heard a man nearby say, "Hi."

I didn't recognize the voice, but presumably he was talking to me as there wasn't anyone else around. I looked over the rims of my magnifiers and saw ten hairy toes protruding from a pair of flip flops. Like a hobbits', if hobbits wore flip flops. Deciding it was rude to stare at someone's feet, I looked up to see a Sasquatch. Seriously. This guy had a fuzzy, curly, blond pelt from head to toe. It's easy to tell when it's mid-July, and everyone's in tank tops and shorts. A little voice in my head snickered, and queried, "Lycanthropy?" I told it to quit being a jerk and shut up.

"Hi," I said. Furry or not, he had beautiful blue eyes, clear and crystalline. Otherwise, well, guys who need curry combs just weren't my type.

"Can I join you?" he asked.

"If you like," I said, scooting over to

give him room. Polite enough, anyway.

"I think I know who you are. Joc from Lock & Key?"

"That's right," I said. "I can't say the same about you, though." I smiled the kind of smile you give someone you've just met.

His teeth were barely visible through his heavy mustache as he smiled back. "Not surprised. Seeing a friend, don't live here, though." He gave me the impression of a bird fluffing itself up to make itself look bigger, trying to impress a prospective mate. "I'm a contractor from out of town. Name's Randy."

"Nice to meet you."

And then, he did something odd. He put out his hand as if expecting me to shake it, even though I hadn't stopped stitching except for occasional glances in his direction. "Most people would shake hands, Joc." His tone was scolding, and it set my teeth on edge.

"I have to be very careful to keep my hands and work clean," I replied, keeping my voice neutral, but inwardly I was starting to seethe. Who did he think he was? My mother?

He changed direction. "So, how's Tim?"

Completely caught off guard, all of my alarm bells started to sound. "How do you know Tim?" I asked casually. What the hell?

He shrugged. "College."

We all went to the same school. News to me. Thankfully, I seemed to have left no imprint.

But then he looked at me more closely. Oh, crap.

He scooched forward on the seat and pointed at me. "Hey! I remember you! You hung out with my old college pal sometimes!"

I shrugged. "Don't remember." It was the truth. In those days, I was almost entirely focused on my studies and didn't have room for much of a social life. Tim and I were Lit study partners, and it was he who brought me into theater life. I helped him with his lines, and when the director found out I did artsy stuff, he handed me a paint brush and put me to work on sets. I loved the work and enjoyed the people. My idea of partying was hanging out with the theater gang once a week after Friday rehearsal, drinking beer and noshing pizza before slamming into the books again.

Randy switched gears. "Is he married?" He laughed. "Are you?"

I stopped dead and stared at him, shocked. "Excuse me?"

"Are you two an item? People talk, you know." He winked conspiratorially at me.

I had had quite enough of him and his games. I packed everything up, tucking them neatly away in my workbag. Putting the bag over my shoulder, I turned to go. "Good night," I said.

I hoped he wouldn't follow me but didn't have the nerve to turn and look back.

EIGHTEEN

Of course, Randy the Weird showed up at the shop the next day.

I saw him coming from across the street. "Oh no."

"What?" Tim looked up from some stock he was receiving.

I pointed.

"Oh shit," he said.

Tim, not being the sort to use invective without just cause, turned his face into the very model of professional welcome as Randy stepped in.

"Hey, how's my old college buddy?"

he boomed enthusiastically. "Hi, Joc!"

I nodded at him.

Tim has a thing that he does when he is going into a role. I call it his "prelude." He will look at something–in this instance, our counter––for a couple of seconds and settle in. Today's scene was "Old College Pals Reunite." I had a feeling that the scene playing inside his head was far different.

"Hi, Randy, what a surprise!" he said cheerfully. Tim could do fake effusive really, really well when he had to. "Good to see you. How have you been?"

It had the effect he was hoping for. Randy seemed startled by his burst of friendliness and paused for a moment. "Oh, good, good. Terrific, in fact. Looks like you've done okay."

"Yup," Tim said. "What brings you our way?"

"My girl lives here."

"Nice," Tim said.

So far, the conversation had been small talk, all neutral. But that was about to change.

"Well…" Randy leaned on the counter and paused. Cleared his throat. Fidgeted. Stood up straight again. "It's been a while since college, hasn't it?"

"Not really," Tim said. His tone was more than affable, but his words clearly made Randy nervous, as did his patience. Tim could outwait anyone when he felt the need. "What's up?"

Randy decided it was prudent to back up a few feet. "I wanted to tell you… I was a jerk in college."

"Yeah?" His voice was calm. His face gave nothing away.

Randy twitched. "Yeah. I just wanted to say I'm sorry."

"That's very decent of you," Tim said. He was blank slating Randy right into flight mode.

"Um, okay. That's all I wanted to say. I gotta go now."

"Have a nice day," Tim said pleasantly as Randy hurried out the door.

The bell jangled.

"Okay, give," I said, as the actor disappeared back into my friend. "How come I don't know anything about this? And what was all that about?"

"I never talked about it because I just wanted to forget it. Didn't have the space in my head for it, to be honest. No time either. Too distracting. You, ma'am, have just met the most annoying ex-college roommate on the face of the planet."

"I think I need to sit down for this," I said, taking a stool. "So you were roomies?"

Tim sighed. "For about five minutes. Really, for two months that lasted a decade."

I made a face. "That good, huh?"

"You don't know the half of it. A real slob. Not just with his stuff-–he'd move mine around too if he thought it was in his way. The capper was when I came back to the dorm one afternoon to finish work on my Lit paper, only to discover that he'd taken all of my notes and reference books-–all arranged in order on my desk-–and apparently scooped them up and dumped them haphazardly all over my bed. A lot of them fell on the floor, of course, and a bunch of bookmarks fell out. I walked in to find him thumbing through my notes and putting papers wherever he felt like it."

"Oh boy," I breathed.

"Would you like to know what he put on my desk?"

"I shudder to think."

"His dirty laundry."

I leaned forward on one elbow,

cocked an eyebrow. "And he lived?"

"Barely. He saw the look in my eyes and ran out of there fast." He shook his head at the memory. "I don't think I've ever been so mad in my life."

"How come I never heard anything about this?" I asked.

"I didn't want you looking for him or him accidentally latching on to you."

"I appreciate that," I said.

"And get this. He *shed*."

Maybe my evil little voice hadn't been so wrong after all.

"So what happened?"

"I went down to Student Housing to see what could be done about him, only to be shown a note which had been flung onto the front counter as its writer fled the scene. The admin was trying not to laugh as she handed it to me."

"What did it say?"

"'Help! My roommate is going to

murder me! Randy Granger.'"

"Well, that was succinct," I said.

"Yup. I had calmed down by then and told her what had happened over the last two months and that I was seeking a divorce. She said not to worry about it, that she would get him rehomed by nightfall, and have the RA gather all his stuff in our dorm room and store it in his office for pick up. I said that sounded great, because my working theory at the time was that Randy might have figured I'd clean up after him, and if he put his homicidal roommate to work as a maid, he'd be more likely to survive the next twenty-four hours."

"Why did you get to stay?"

"That's what I asked. She said everyone liked me right where I was. With Randy out of the picture, I did too."

"What happened to Randy? Where'd he end up?"

"You know, I never asked. Then again, every time he saw me, he'd go the other way."

I was not surprised. "What happened to you? Did you get another roommate?"

"Sure did. It turned out there was a Junior who'd just transferred in and needed a place to stay. We hit it off. He was a year behind me. Great roommate."

"That's great." I straightened. "You know, though? I don't trust that guy. Something about him really bothers me. Like he owns women."

"No mystery there," Tim said. "He's always been that way. Some ladies were okay with it at school. Most weren't. But if his girlfriend likes it, that's between them."

"The mystery woman."

"Yes. And she can just stay that way."

I couldn't have agreed more.

NINETEEN

A few days went by in relative peace for us, but it was very different in the Martin home. Johnny refused to talk to his father, and Marion and Rich barely spoke at all.

One evening when Johnny had gone over to Bobby's and Marion having asked Ellen to keep him for an hour or two, she and Rich had it out in the middle of their kitchen. It was less a fight than it was a realization of what she'd endured for the last eleven years. She said he'd called her a drama queen and was sick of her histrionics, but the truth of the matter was that she was sick and tired of *him*. There was no forgiving his behavior. Not this time.

"So, you eventually decided to come home, smelling of your playmates? Were you hanging out with them instead of getting on a plane and being there for your family?"

Rich retaliated just like she thought he might. "Like I don't know you're having an affair with that theater director? Yeah, explain that one to me, Marion! Like why you're gone twice, three times a week for hours at a time? Do you think I'm stupid?"

"Do you think I am? Since when are you here to notice?" she snapped.

"Well, maybe if I had a wife who showed me a little affection from time to time..."

"I call bullshit, Rich. Do you think I

cook and clean for fun?"

"Taking care of me is your job," he said.

"Works both ways. So do our marriage vows. Instead, I get to do your laundry every week. All I can say about yours lately is that it's been educational."

"What about your lover, that director friend of yours?"

"There is no such person. That theater director and I are friends who are producing a play with a talented bunch of other friends who are together the whole time, and if you ever dropped by the community theater on the nights I was out, you'd know that for a fact."

As Marion said, it was a stalemate.

Rich's cell pinged, and he pulled it from his pocket. There was a text from his boss. "Need you back In Vegas ASAP. Alaska's holding ticket for 5pm flight. Same hotel. Got your old room. Reserved under the company name. Reply Y if you're coming."

Rich tapped the Y key. He showed the text to Marion, glanced at the clock. It was just now 3. "Time for a quick shower and packing," he said. "I have to hurry."

"Do you want me to drive you, or—" Angry or not, she was still practical.

"Call a cab," he said brusquely, and headed upstairs. When he came down a half hour later, bags in hand, he took his keys from the dish by the front door and left without saying goodbye.

Marion had not spoken to Johnny yet about his father. She'd know when it was time. Rich called once to tell them he was in Vegas. "Okay," Marion said curtly, and hung up.

He called right back. "Hey, can I talk

to Johnny?"

Marion looked across the table at her son, who looked up at her from doing his homework. He'd heard his dad's voice. He shook his head. "He's not here right now," she said, and disconnected.

Fuck him, she thought. Her thoughts moved toward a future without him.

It just happened a lot sooner than she'd thought. At two o'clock that morning, a part of her life simply left.

The phone rang. She grabbed it off the nightstand, switched it to speaker. "Hello?" she answered softly, not wanting to disturb her son in the next room. She didn't recognize the number.

A breathy and somewhat inebriated female voice answered. "Hi!" it chirped. "Are you Marion?"

She realized immediately that it

wasn't the police. "Who wants to know?"

"I'm Tawny," the woman purred. "I just wanted to thank you."

Marion sat up straight. So, Peter had been right after all. "Do you have any idea what time it is?"

She heard a giggle. "Of course I do, silly. It's playtime!"

"The rest of the Pacific time zone is asleep! Thank me for what?"

"My boyfriend. He said to call you."

"Really?" By now, Marion's voice had all the warmth of a polar vortex. "Is the *father of our child* there?"

She heard a low male voice in the background. There was no mistaking it.

Tawny giggled. "He's on our nice big heart-shaped bed, tempting me with a nice big *hot* drink. I'm coming, Baby! Just thinking about it. I'm going to su—"

"Tawny!" Marion interrupted

sharply. "I don't want to hear about your activities!"

Tawny was cooing, her voice projected away from the phone. "Ooooooo, you're such a big man, Rich, a real man...."

Marion lowered her voice. It became the hiss of a viper, venomous fangs and all. "Oh Tawny..."

"Yes?" a giggling voice responded.

"Listen up. Your "real man" is too much of a fucking coward to talk to his own wife. No—he made you do it. Think about that, because if you do stay with him, you'll always be doing stuff you don't want to because he hasn't the balls to do it himself."

"Oh, he's got the b—"

A petulant male voice came from the background. "C'mon baby, I need you on these silk sheets right now!"

"Ooooo Rich...." Mercifully, the

connection broke.

Marion put the phone face down on the nightstand and cried. Despite her best efforts to be quiet, Johnny had heard her and crawled into bed with her.

"Was that dad?" he asked.

"Yes, honey," she said, stroking his hair.

Johnny was very perceptive and pieced the parts together quickly. "He's staying in Vegas, isn't he?"

"Yes, baby. Maybe for a long time."

"I'm sorry, Mom."

"You have nothing to be sorry for, sweetie. This is all on him."

The night passed, with low conversation and eventually, sleep.

The next day I went over to Marion's, armed with a box of tissues and a bottle of chardonnay.

"Why is it that when men do something stupid, they expect their women to swoop in and rescue them? I'm so done, Joc! If he really feels that way about us, he can just stay there. As far as money goes, I already moved all the accounts to my name, so we'll be fine. I left him fifteen thousand in the joint account and pulled my name off of it. Little Dick can go do his own thing without using Johnny's college fund. I'm just so tired of him hurting us. Especially Johnny. His father deserted him, and I doubt very much if Johnny will ever forgive him for that. I know I won't."

"What will you do if he calls?"

Marion's demeanor was fierce. "Tell him to go to hell. Sin City can keep him."

It was only then that she reached for a tissue and ended up sobbing in my arms.

That night, she called me at home. "I called Peter," she said.

I'd suspected she would. Marion was one of those people who would respect her marriage vows until all respect was gone. "What did you tell him?

"I'm free."

TWENTY

A few nights later, the cast was given a rest, and the set people were called in to do a full inspection of the stage. Tim decided to accompany me in case they needed an extra pair of hands. Ed showed up with his tool bag. Marion arrived, typically loaded with her stuff bag containing anything and everything one could ever possibly need for a quick repair or a tweak. Tonight, she was armed with carpet needles and heavy-duty thread.

Cam, training under Peter, was

learning how to maintain a theater. Peter looked at the stage and asked Cam to help him close the curtains. "Okay, let's inspect them," he said and went up the side stairs to the catwalk, Cam following. Each carried a piece of chalk to mark trouble spots and a flashlight so they could do a detailed inspection.

Cam started at stage left, Peter at stage right. They would meet in the middle where the curtains intersected. The inner curtains being in perfect shape, Peter called down to have them drawn all the way open. Then they started on the heavy outer curtains. The fabric was held up by sturdy metal grommets, covered and oversewn so they wouldn't show. They were built to last decades, given proper care, and had in fact been in use for the last twenty years or so. They were a beautiful thick golden velvet, kept nice by periodic vacuuming and brushing.

The guys took up their positions, got down on all fours. Cam looked at the first grommet, stopped, pulled out his flashlight and looked again. "Mr. Fokes?" he asked. His brow was furrowed in a very unCamlike fashion.

Peter had just pulled his flashlight out to start his end. Coming over, he saw what Cam was pointing at. "Marion, get up here!" He sounded horrified.

She grabbed a flashlight and shoved it in her shorts pocket, all but running up onto the catwalk. "What in the–?" On her hands and knees, she crawled down the line, stopping at each grommet. "Oh, my God."

"What do you see?" Peter called.

"The same thing. Every single grommet." She looked like she was about to cry.

The curtains had been sliced most of the way around each grommet, all the way through the thick fabric. The curtains were fraying significantly as their weight and gravity pulled them down. That they would fall sooner rather than later was obvious, and when they did, it was likely to be in a rush, a domino effect, the weight of each pleat pulling down the others. There was nothing to arrest the fall. That they still clung on was a miracle, and one not expected to last.

She looked at Peter, horror in her eyes.

Peter and Marion were an item, but not in the usual way. The place which had brought them together was a neglected auditorium which had been many things over the years. The building itself was over one hundred years old, and had served as a courthouse, a church, a theater, and an assembly house. Whoever'd built it had terraced the floor, and as the seats weren't bolted down, the space was easy to adapt to any number of uses.

By the time Peter found it, shortly after moving here, it had been abandoned for a while, and the town was wondering what to do with it. He attended a town meeting where this was discussed, and before he knew it, he and Marion, a regular who'd lived there a few years longer than he had, had been wondering the same thing, and before they knew it, they were almost tripping each other up in their eagerness. The town council gave them the go-ahead and the money to have the building inspected, and two total strangers found themselves embroiled in their passion for the theater. They picked through every nook and cranny of the place, coming at last to a set of cupboards in what would later become our prop room. As one, they pulled the doors open.

There, covered in the thin plastic bags used by dry cleaners, were some huge neatly folded up pieces of sheer black fabric. One by one, they put them on the floor and carefully unwrapped them. It didn't take long to determine that they were inner stage curtains.

They then opened the adjacent cupboard and found the heavy gold velvet curtains which could only be the primary drapes. They were not in the best of shape. The hems were frayed in a few places, and the velvet had settled from incorrect storage. They needed desperately to be mended and steamed and brushed, the cartridge pleats reshaped.

Although the fabrics were warped from being folded and sitting so long–

who really knew how long they'd been there? —and smelling a bit musty from not being aired for a long while, they could be made usable again with some expert TLC. Marion, herself a theater major with contacts just about everywhere, whisked them off to have them refurbished, and had taken immaculate care of them ever since. While she always deferred to Peter as the stage manager and director, he always deferred to her as the keeper of the curtains. No one at the theater doubted that for a second.

And now her babies had been raped.

"What do you think?" Peter asked. His eyes were stormy. Marion wiped her eyes and pulled herself together.

"We can't use them in this

condition," she said. "There's no time to order replacements, but I'll see what I can do. The damage is way too extensive to fix with spit and duct tape." She looked at the damage nearest her. "We have to drop them, Peter. Nothing to do but take them down completely. It's too dangerous to leave them up."

He nodded. "Okay. Everyone down there, move the props to the back of the stage, then clear off. I want you all at least midway up the aisle in front of house when we drop these. Everyone will be present and accounted for. No exceptions. Cam, Ed, Tim—-you're with me. Joc, we all need utility knives. All right, let's do this."

So armed, they all went up to the catwalk. Peter asked for another head count just to be safe. Everyone was present and accounted for. Two guys to each curtain, one on either end. "All right. We're going to do a controlled drop. When you reach the middle of the drape, call out. We'll release them one at a time." They carefully cut the curtains away from their fraying supports.

The last cuts were made. First, the left drape, then the right. The curtains fell in a hapless pile, spilling over the stage into the front rows.

Marion hopped up on stage. There she knelt and examined the bottom edge of the curtains. Her babies were wounded, but there was no way they were going down without a fight.

"What do you think?" Peter asked.

She pulled part of a hem up to show him. "We've got a good foot of hem here, and the seams are in good shape. I think if we turn the curtains around and use the bottoms as the tops, we should be okay. We'd still have to have them professionally equipped and sewn, though."

"Okay," he said. "That will still leave us with a deficit of three feet."

"I've been thinking about that. Once the damaged binding is removed, we could make it up by adding a new bottom, maybe velvet, maybe something else. A new color could also be in contrast to this gold. Maybe something not so Classical and stuffy—red and black have been done to death! But it would be a lot less expensive than replacing both curtains and would look quite nice."

He smiled. "Great idea. I leave you to your magical connections." Then, far more seriously, he said, "I want to call in the sheriff."

She looked deeply into his eyes. "I think you should."

TWENTY-ONE

Steven came over almost immediately. He took in the lot of us and the heaped piles of golden velvet. "Well, this is a mess," he said. "What do you think happened?"

I spoke up for the first time. "I think it's possible that they were vandalized with a utility knife."

"Why's that?"

"A couple of things. Utility knives have scales for a good grip. Prints don't show. And they're all over the place here. We're constantly using them for one thing or another."

"Did you look for prints on the velvet?"

Marion laid her hand flat on a section, removed it. All she'd done was leave a slight discoloration from disturbing the pile.

"All right then," Steven said. "Let's assume that this was done while no one else was in the building. Who has the keys?"

"I do," Peter said. "So does Marion. I sometimes loan mine to Cam when he comes in and does odd jobs around the place, but he always returns them on time. He hasn't been in here alone for the past week. Corrine, our costumer, same thing. And of course, there's Gavin."

Gavin Richards was a gifted local artist. He made a good living at it. He was also one of the theater's biggest fans and had been volunteering his time and talents to its beautification as a gift to the town. The once plain foyer now held Classical sconces on the walls, laurel vines cascading down them, so real you swore you could touch them, but all you would feel was a wall. Gavin loved doing *trompe l'oeil*—that amazing style dating back to antiquity which creates the illusion of depth. He continued to add splendor to the place and was currently working on a row of Greek columns for inside the theater proper.

"What about Gavin?"

"He comes and goes as he pleases. Have you seen his latest designs? Utterly mind-blowing. He loves it here—there's no way he would ever do anything to hurt the place."

"So that rules out everyone who should have keys," Steven said. "When do you think this was done?"

"Had to have been in the last day or two," Peter replied. "Everyone took a much-needed break."

"And the curtains would agree with that timeline," Marion said.

"What makes you say that?" Steven asked.

"I know my fabrics," she said, looking him in the eye. "And how much those curtains weigh. The rate at which they were tearing seems to match my calculations. Another few days and they would've fallen on their own. Which could have been disastrous if they'd come down in the middle of rehearsal." She shuddered.

Tim said, "Talk about a surreptitious act of violence."

Steven looked at him. "What makes you say that?"

"Have you ever been smacked by an out-of-control stage curtain?"

"No, but couldn't you just crawl out from under it?"

"Of course," Marion said. "If you have the presence of mind and can deal with the weight. I've seen this sort of thing before. It can be like being buried under an avalanche. People tend to panic and panic leads to injuries."

"Plus, there's always the added danger of them hitting props, which in our case includes walls," Peter added. "You can always minimize the risks--lighter materials and so forth--but if a wall comes down on you, it's going to hurt, and there's no way around that. Domino effects on stage aren't pretty."

"And how do we know that the person who did this wasn't planning on having them fall during a performance? Like opening night?" Marion added, worry in her voice.

Steven took one last look at the

curtains. "Okay. We'll keep our eyes out for any suspicious behavior, and you do the same."

"Thanks," Peter said.

As Steven rose, we all picked up a portion of curtain at Marion's direction and began the task of neatly folding them up, one pleat at a time. Steven stayed where he was and observed our operations.

TWENTY-TWO

Marion did indeed work her magic. She called in some favors from her old college friends in the drama department who set to work right away.

A few nights later, Tim and I met her in the parking lot of the theater. She was dragging a massive box from the back of her car onto her hand truck. We jumped in right away and helped her maneuver the awkward load into place. It took the three of us to keep it balanced as we rolled it down the center aisle and heaved it onto the stage floor. Back we ran for the other box.

Peter, on stage at the time, was watching all of this with great amusement. "Christmas, Marion?"

"Much better!" she exclaimed, grinning. Tim and I raised the boxes' lids so that they made no contact with the contents, and Marion very carefully split them open with her utility knife, revealing masses of neatly folded fabric wrapped in cellophaned glory. "Our curtains!" she exclaimed in triumph.

Everyone came running, regardless of where they were. "We should hang them," she said. "The fabric needs to relax." With any luck, their own weight would take out any creases. On Marion's instructions, we unpacked them and formed a line, snaking them up the stairs and across the catwalk. Peter, Tim, Cam, and Ed hung them up while we ladies fed them to the guys as needed. Marion was down on stage on a sturdy ladder, shaking out the top of each pleat once it was securely hung, with me doing the adjustments at the bottom. The gracefully rolled pleats cooperated and hung straight.

Peter gave the all-clear and recommended that everyone get out to the seats to get the full effect. On cue, he and Cam opened them, then slowly drew them closed, where they hung beautifully. We all ooo'd and ahh'd.

Marion had been so right to suggest the changes she did. The curtains had been a bit plain before, but now they were nothing short of elegant. Rather than replace the fabric with a "stuffy" color, as Marion called it, they now were a beautiful shade of teal, the top being a wide border of the old but noble curtains, refurbished and looking like new.

And the new fabric wasn't just matte. This stuff was gorgeous-—a heavy plush fabric with a rich brocaded pattern. I have no idea who exactly Marion called, but whoever it was must have had ties to the garment district to find something so opulent.

Peter and Cam parted them again to show the whole effect, closing the inner drapes first, then the outer. Everyone applauded and cheered. The action was perfect, the curtains beautiful. "I think we owe you pizza after this," Peter said.

"At the very least," she replied flirtatiously. Everyone laughed.

"Pizza or burrito?" Tim asked as he drove us home.

"Burrito, I think," I said. "No woman gives a man a look like that unless she wants to be rolled up with all the toppings."

My rather flip remark had a grain of

truth in it. Anyone with eyes could tell that she and Peter were great friends, but to think beyond that was best kept as private speculation. One Mrs. Holbrook was quite enough!

TWENTY-THREE

Randy was still hanging around town. Normally, this wouldn't have bothered me at all. But he refused to leave me alone and that was worrisome. Mostly, it was annoying.

Not that I felt he was inherently dangerous. He was a pest. If we happened to bump into each other anywhere--the market, the park, the shop--he always tried to push me. At least, he hadn't invaded the theater yet, thank God! As long as he stayed hands off, I could deal with him.

It always started innocently enough. "Hi, Jocelyn," he'd say.

"Hi, Randy," I'd respond, just to be polite. If I was doing something, I'd glance up briefly to acknowledge him and then go back to whatever I was working on. I never even so much as smiled at the guy.

He came to the shop for one reason only—to get under our skins. He'd drift around the shelves and pick at the displays to give himself an air of legitimacy. He'd say hi to Tim and then avoid him.

Tim admitted to me that having Randy around gave him the willies. The guy was just weird. We decided to keep an eye on him.

But Randy never took the hint. He'd

try to engage me in small talk, and I wouldn't let him. Eventually, he'd say something like, "Hey, you want to go out to dinner with me?"

"No, Randy. I don't."

"You like playing hard to get, don't you?" He'd flex his chest and arm muscles, putting on some sort of fuzzy testosterone-fueled display. It had all the appearance of tribbles in the throes of *gran mal* epileptic seizures. "Whaddya think?"

"I think I'm not interested," I'd say firmly. "I mean it, Randy. Lay off."

"Lots of ladies would love to get what you're getting."

"Fine. Go bother them." I tried to sound neutral and calm, I swear I did. "Starting with your girlfriend."

His face reddened. "It's Tim, isn't it?"

I knew it. The feud wasn't over yet.

Only this time I was the prize. I just had no plans on becoming collateral damage.

"What the hell are you talking about?"

The last line was Tim's. He'd slipped in quietly next to me, unnoticed by Randy or me. He'd observed the whole exchange. He looked from me to Randy and back again. "You okay, Joc?"

"So far," I said. "Look Randy, I'm not into you. I never will be into you. You're not my type. Now do us all a favor and go away."

He moved toward the door, opened it, and fired a parting shot across the bow. Voice full of macho bravado, he looked at me and said, "It's your loss."

"Not even," I replied coldly. As the door closed behind Randy, Tim saw the fury rising in my eyes and thought it best to deflect it.

"Criminy," he said. "Is he ever going

to leave town? I feel like shooting him sometimes."

"It's illegal to hunt Bigfoot in this state," I said, and we both fell apart laughing.

But Randy wouldn't let up, and both of us were becoming increasingly concerned. Tim caught Randy outside one day and stopped him. He wanted witnesses. "Look, Randy," he said, "how you feel toward Jocelyn is none of my business, but I will tell you this. She's not interested in you, and she never will be. If you keep bugging her, I will know, and I will take steps to see that you stop. Are we clear?"

Randy was taller than Tim, but my partner's stage presence made him seem like he was looking down on Randy.

"Yeah, sure," the latter said easily and walked away.

We both knew that wouldn't be the end of it, unfortunately. And sure enough, Randy took it as a personal challenge and an affront to his manhood that must be avenged.

Later that day, he came back into the shop while Tim was out on an errand, made a beeline for me, and the next thing I knew, I was being smothered in fuzz as he attempted to force my mouth open and rape my tongue.

I broke free, stepped back, and swung my fist full force, clocking him one across the cheek. I heard something crack. "Don't you ever, *ever* touch me again!" I knew I yelled as loudly as I could, but it didn't seem loud enough.

My blow had knocked him back several feet. He rubbed his face, saw blood on his hand. "You're a tough girl, aren't you?" He started to advance on me. His eyes were scaring me. There was a look there that made me shiver.

Fear was rapidly replaced by an adrenalin-fueled rage. How dare this sorry ass excuse for a human being think he had any rights when it came to me? I stood my ground, the power pulsing through my body, ready to become an inferno.

I stared him down, eyes narrowed, set to pounce.

"Bitch!" he snarled and stepped forward. "You like it rough, don't you?"

He was stopped abruptly when someone yanked his arms back, cuffing him. "I saw the whole thing from the street. You okay, Jocelyn?"

"Yes, Steven, thanks." I was starting to tremble, trying to hold myself together. I did not want that Sasquatch to see my reaction!

"He and I are going to have a nice little talk, and I think he'll be staying for the slumber party."

I managed a feeble smile, and they left. Randy had been caught so off guard that he went out as meekly as a comatose kitten. It wasn't until the car door slammed after him that he started talking to Steven, but what was said, I couldn't hear. It looked loud, though.

When Tim returned a few minutes later, he found me sitting cross-legged on the floor, crying and shaking with repressed fear and shock, the excess adrenalin leaving my system. My hand hurt. Without a word, he shut the shop door, flipped the sign to "Closed," and let me sob on his shoulder until I was all cried out.

When it was over, I went to the restroom to wash my face and tidy up and came back to Tim holding out a steaming cup to me. It didn't smell like caffeine.

"What's this?"

"Chamomile tea."

"I hate chamomile tea."

"I know you do, but you need it now. Please." His gentle expression was impossible to turn down. I took the cup, sipped.

"Darn your puppy dog eyes," I said.

He grinned at me.

"This is actually good."

"I made it strong, just for you."

Was there such a thing as strong chamomile tea? Because if there was, this was yummy. I sat back in an armchair and let the calm overtake me.

Tim knew I'd been mugged once. I'd tried to fight my way out of it and lost, but not before leaving a number of identifying marks on the creeps who did it. In retrospect, I should've just thrown my wallet in their direction and run for it while they were distracted. But I don't have a victim mentality, and running away from the confrontation never even entered my mind.

Fortunately, all the thugs wanted was money, and since I wasn't carrying any, they took out their frustrations on me. I wasn't raped, but the bruises lasted for weeks. It was one of the reasons I'd wanted to leave the city to start a business, to live somewhere where you could trust the people on the street to look out for you as you'd look out for them, and predators stood a much higher chance of getting trapped and dealt with like the human vermin they were. That was what we had here, and we loved it.

Thinking back on it, I believe I could have beaten Randy into a pudding, and the law and the town would have made sure I never caught so much as a glimpse of the inside of a jail cell.

TWENTY-FOUR

That night at rehearsal Marion slipped me a little cylinder of pepper spray. "Get the son of a bitch," she murmured. "Then send him to me." Her expression broached no argument as to what would happen to Randy once he was delivered.

"How did you know?" I hadn't said a word to anyone.

"Tim told me." She grinned. "Warrior women!" We high-fived, and I tucked the Randy deterrent into my pocket.

Mrs. Holbrook was so cheerful she could have been on holiday--there was so much exciting stuff happening! The story of the bookshop owner who beat the crap out of the mysterious stranger who attacked her. The stranger getting kicked out of town. The theater curtains. A couple headed for divorce and a love affair between the attractive wife and the handsome theater director. It was all too good not to share.

Mrs. Holbrook obviously under-estimated Marion Martin.

She was hanging out with her gaggle outside of the grocery store as usual. Marion, who just happened to be passing by, noted that at least they weren't blocking the door.

"Oh my goodness, you'll *never* believe this. I know I didn't at first, but my word! Have you heard about Peter Fokes and Marion Martin?"

Everyone said they hadn't and leaned in breathlessly for more.

"They're *lovers* now! Rich Martin went to work in Vegas, and she—well, *she* didn't waste any time!"

"My God, Lizzy, you must lead such a boring life to make up these fantasies about other people."

Everyone started, none more so than Elizabeth Holbrook. Her eyes narrowed and her upper lip curled into an ugly expression, her gay demeanor completely shattered. She hated being called Lizzy.

She hated even more when someone called her out. And here was this upstart theater person, the current focus of her attention, her expression calm and cool, doing just that!

"Well Marion, what have *you* to say

for yourself?" she countered.

"One of these days, someone is going to sue you." She may as well have been reciting the alphabet.

With that, Marion carried on, leaving a gape-faced Mrs. Holbrook in the dust.

She and Peter spent a lot of time together, she told me. Very little of it was personal—they'd decided to save all that until after the play. That they enjoyed each other's company and made a fantastic team was obvious. It had been obvious for the last two years.

For the company, it was business as usual.

As for Mrs. Holbrook, she marched forward, speaking in italics like always.

TWENTY-FIVE

The following morning, Tim and I were at the shop early as usual when Cam showed up at the door with the Bichons. I waved and let them in, relocking the door. Tim offered Cam some coffee, which he accepted. They went into the office, Cam carrying the store water bowl.

Taking the dogs off leash, I sat down in one of the armchairs. K2 and Matt leaped onto my lap, wagging their tails furiously and attempting to lick me to death. I was giggling and cooing some nonsense at them when the guys joined me. "So, Cam," I asked, "to what do we owe the pleasure?"

Tim put the water bowl on the floor for the dogs and they hopped down to enthusiastically lap at it.

Cam handed me a coffee. A possible peace offering before he sprang something on me I might not like? I was intrigued.

"Well," he said, "I talked it over with Tim and Mom and Dad, and we all agree. You need some ferocious guard dogs until that Randy prick leaves town."

Verbal slip aside, I could not have been more surprised. "What makes you think that they'd—?"

"Oh, they hate him," Cam said decisively. "I was walking them at the park the other day when we crossed paths and both of them went nuts. Barking, growling, snapping, the works.

He yelled at me for having such vicious dogs, and I told him to back down or I'd let them remove his ankles."

"My little champions," I cooed, reaching over and ruffling both dogs. They grinned toothily at me.

"There's something off with that guy, and they know it."

It seemed like a lot of us reacted that way to Randy.

"Cam and I think this is an excellent idea," Tim said. "What do you think?"

"Conspirators. Traitors. Can't let a self-respecting girl beat the crap out of a moron who totally deserves it," I teased, dodging a doggy French kiss. "I love the idea. Thanks, guys."

There was a knock at the door. A man stood there patiently. He was one of our regulars. John…John something. The coffee hadn't hit yet. Then it did. My eyes focused. Seamus. John Seamus. He was an older man, slender, with long silver hair neatly tied back in a ponytail. His sparkling blue eyes were intelligent and kind. He'd charmed my socks off from the first moment I met him. If I wore socks.

I glanced at the clock. Ten minutes to go. What the heck. I nodded at Tim.

Tim unlocked the door, turned the sign to "Open. Good morning," he said. "Please come on in."

John looked up at the clock. "Oh, dear. I'm early. Are you sure it's no bother?"

I stood up, dumping the dogs off my lap. "Don't be silly," I said. "How are you, John?"

Before he could reply, the Bichons trotted side by side over to him and sat down in front of him like perfect little gentlemen. "Oh, aren't you two charmers," he said, holding out his hand so they could smell him. He gave them each a pat. "Your shop dogs? How come we've never met?"

I grinned at Cam, and he gave me a thumbs-up.

"They visit us from time to time," Tim said.

"I'll have to come by more often," John said. "Lovely fellows, aren't you?"

"To what do we owe the honor?" I asked, gesturing to a chair.

John took it. "Well, I wanted to ask my favorite purveyors of mayhem and mystery about something. Some friends and I are interested in starting a book club. Specifically, a mystery book club."

"Very cool," I said. "How can we help?"

"Well, there's just three of us right now, myself and two friends, but we were thinking we might try to work out something with you to build our membership and enhance your delightful business."

"We're listening," Tim said. "What are you thinking?"

"Well...we were wondering if you might be interested in doing an open house, something of that sort."

We both nodded. That could be very effective. We could do it the week after the play closed. Have a kind of evening reception, with coffee and cookies. Showcase certain titles. This could be a lot of fun. I might even have the mantelpiece embroidery done by then— we could even debut it! It was getting close to done now, and I hoped to frame it in a week or two.

"It sounds wonderful," I said. "Let's do it."

Tim offered John a latte. A half hour later, we were toasting to our mutual success.

TWENTY-SIX

Steven asked us to come down to his office that afternoon. It being a slow day, we decided to close early and went over around four.

Randy had been released with a warning. Namely, to knock off the crap or his little overnight stay might become something longer. I'd decided not to press charges on the grounds that maybe a night in jail would be warning enough. If it weren't, there would be hell to pay, and it would all land on him. I'll forgive stupid, but only once.

"So, what happened?" I asked.

"I ran a background check on him," Steven began. "Nothing stands out."

"But what's he doing here?" Tim asked. "He told us he was a private contractor."

"Oh, he is. I talked to his boss, who wasn't too happy with him."

"Why's that?" Tim asked.

"Because he was supposed to report in last night and didn't. Boss needed him back today. I cut him loose and sent him back to work."

"Does his boss know why he was in jail?"

"I said that he was in for a D&D and was here sleeping it off. No reason to drag you into it."

"Thank you," I said.

"What does he do?" Tim asked.

"He's a builder, does roofing."

I looked at my partner. "He came

looking for you."

"And he found you. Dammit!"

His frustration was touching. "It's not your fault," I said. "That's entirely on him."

Steven looked at both of us. "And your stage curtains?"

We were stuck again. There's no way Randy could have done it. Access was the one thing he didn't have. And why would he want to sabotage a stage production? If there was a motive there, it remained entirely elusive.

"Where is he now?" I asked.

"He promised me he was headed back to Portland. As far as I know, he should be there by now." He picked up his cell, punched in a number. "Hello, is this Green Roofing? ... Great. This is Sheriff Danielson. Yes, the guy who kept one of your crew overnight. Did Randy Granger report in today? ... Yes, just following up. ... He's out on a job with a crew? ... Great. Thank you." He punched out, looked up at us. "Okay," he said. "I hope that's the end of it."

"Us, too," we said. "Thank you, Sheriff."

As we left, our anxiety left with us, treading on our heels. What the hell was going on?

"Hey, Tim," I said, just to change the subject, "You'll never guess what that idiot said to me."

"Something idiotic?" he hazarded.

I laughed. I was suddenly nervous and couldn't quite figure out why. Nervous around Tim? "I'm not so sure. He wanted to know if we're an item."

He paused mid-step. "What do you think?"

"I think I have the best friend and business partner anyone could ever want."

"Very mutual," he said. "Have you ever thought about going further?"

"Why? Do you want to?" Sex didn't scare me but ruining a relationship over it did. I didn't want those complications. Having a trusted friend meant far more to me.

"Joc, I'm all guy. I'd have to be stupid not to notice how attractive you are, let alone your personality and talents and crazy skill set. I love how tough you are and how tender. I love having you as my best friend and partner. I trust you more than I trust anyone, including my own family. We're a great team, the two of us. But lovers? It would be like incest."

"I feel the same way," I said. "Now come here and give your favorite friend a hug."

He happily obliged. I leaned up and whispered in his ear, and he cracked up.

Holding hands, we skipped the rest

of the way down the street, headed for cold beer and hot pizza.

Let Mrs. Holbrook chew on that!

TWENTY-SEVEN

Back at the theater, Susan opened her office desk as she always did, reached in for some papers as she always did, her eyes focused on her adversary like always, and screamed.

Ed reached her first, Tim and Peter not far behind.

Her hand was a bruised and bleeding mess, made so by the rat trap attached to it.

Peter yelled for the first aid kit. Being backstage at the time, I ran and got it.

The trap had come down on four of

her fingers. Susan was as white as a sheet, crying. "Get it off," she whispered, tears cascading down her face.

Tim said gently, "Honey, we can't— we could make it worse. Shock, you know? Let's get you to the hospital where they can safely remove it." He took a handkerchief from his pocket and carefully dabbed her face.

I broke the seal on a small ice pack to activate it and handed it to Peter. He placed it as lightly as he could across her knuckles.

He said, "Susan, don't move your hand. Let the EMTs handle it."

She nodded, sniffling in pain. "Who would do this?" she asked. "*Why*?"

"Let's not worry about that now," Tim said. "You're more important."

Marion had punched in 9-1-1 the instant she heard Peter call for the kit. We heard sirens coming toward us. They stopped. Cam ran to the front door and let them in.

"It's okay," Peter soothed. "Help is here. You'll have it off in no time."

Susan whimpered, but nodded and gave him a brave little smile.

As the EMTs worked on her, I returned the first aid kit to its shelf. I could have sworn I heard something akin to a sob, but where it came from, I could not be certain.

A cruel prank, or an outright attack?

Damn my suspicious mind!

Corrine joined me. There were tears in her eyes. "Is Susan going to be okay?" she asked.

"I think so," I said. "Did you see what happened?"

"I heard her scream but didn't see anything. What happened?"

I told her.

"This is horrible!" she exclaimed.

"Who would do such a terrible thing?" Not waiting for an answer, she fetched her purse. "I'm going to the hospital to be with her," she said.

I nodded. "Please give her my best."

My questions persisted and were posed to Peter and Ed when they returned from the hospital.

Susan was being kept overnight. The trap hadn't broken anything but had caused a massive hematoma that needed monitoring and required her to be on something stronger than aspirin for the next twenty-four hours. When they left her, she was sleeping comfortably, her hand wrapped in ice bags.

Back at the theater, the first thing Marion did was check a bit of backstage inventory. No public building is completely free of vermin—the two go hand in hand. Marion said that while she felt for their plight and really didn't begrudge them their desire to be somewhere dry and warm, the critters chewed on everything, and that she would not stand for. She hated the idea of poison traps and believed in quick, humane killing, so she'd invested in a dozen spring-loaded traps and put them in a clear plastic bin labeled in great big letters "RAT TRAPS. NOT A PROP!"

Two of the traps were gone. One Marion herself had set, having noticed a rat behind the theater crawling around the prop room trash bin near the back door. The other, presumably, was the one which had been removed from Susan's hand.

We were all sitting around the stage, Peter on Susan's desk. He was shaking his head in disbelief. "It had to be someone in the company," he said. "Someone who knew she would open that drawer."

"Prints?" I suggested.

"Maybe. But I doubt there's anything clean enough." A roll of clear packing tape magically appeared in his hand. He carefully laid the tape across the drawer handle, lifted it, and stuck the ends to the desk. He also did the same to that side of the desk, then the chair. Marion pulled out her flashlight, and we held the strips up to the light. As Peter had suggested, they were covered in smudges, and there was no distinguishing anything.

"Fuck it!" he exploded and excused himself abruptly. Marion followed, and when I saw them a little later, the rage had died from his eyes and left a deep, cold sadness behind.

"Okay," he said. "Tomorrow. All hands on deck. We're going to have a discussion before we get down to work."

We all nodded.

"Peter—" I started to say, but he stopped me with a hand.

"No more tonight, Joc. Let's go home. Maybe it will make some sense in the morning."

I patted his arm and turned to go. Tim gripped his shoulder. "We'll figure it out," he said, and we left the theater in darkness.

TWENTY-EIGHT

The next day found Susan too unsteady to function yet thanks to the painkillers, and she suggested that her understudy be called in. In addition to being a costumer, Corrine frequently helped many in the company run their lines. She was stage shy, though, she said, and the only reason she'd agreed to be Susan's understudy was because she knew Susan would never need one. Now she was nervous.

"It's just us," Peter said. "Think of it as running lines like you've done a hundred times before."

She took a deep breath and nodded.

She turned out to be quite good. While she lacked Susan's air of imperiousness, she made up for it by projecting a ruthless demeanor. I know I wouldn't have wanted to cross her!

She didn't resemble Susan physically at all. Tall, lean build, dark eyes and hair, carried herself with a natural grace. On stage, she could wear high heels and walk without making a sound, a move Susan had to practice for hours before getting it completely right. Corrine was a cat.

All those years of playing an extra, she said. One learns to be quiet.

Ed Graham, Mr. Rice to her Ms. Dover, said he enjoyed working with her and suggested that she try out for the lead in future plays. "Don't be shy about it," he said. "You're good."

Tim agreed, but he told me privately that he wasn't comfortable with her. There's such a thing as having one's stage character being intimidated. Then there's the real thing. Something about working with Corrine bothered him—he just hoped it was the strangeness of not working with Susan. She was almost as tall as he was, so when they first rehearsed together, he looked where he normally would for Ms. Dover's face only to find her hand tilting his chin toward the ceiling. "I'm up here," she said. Her voice was cool.

Tim blushed furiously and apologized, saying it was just habit and wouldn't happen again. She nodded, and they went on with the scene.

The next time we rehearsed, two nights later, Susan came onstage, complete with bandaged hand, and played her role magnificently. Corrine was nowhere to be found. When I asked Susan about it, she said, "I told her to take the night off. She's really pissed at Tim."

"What?" we both said, surprised.

"Why?" Tim asked. "I thought it went fine. We did have a tiny incident, but it could have happened with anybody."

Susan nodded. "I agree, but according to her, you're a perve for staring at her chest and slobbering all over her décolletage."

"That's ridiculous," Tim said angrily. "I'm amazed she would even suggest it."

Actors in live theater learn fast that bodies are bodies, and so what. A crowded backstage is no place for prudery or prurience. You become immune to skin showing. Even though we have areas curtained off for males and females, there can't help but be occasional glimpses. For Corrine, who costumed and dressed and undressed players of both genders all the time, to say something like this was ludicrous.

It was all too much for Tim. He has a very low tolerance for idiocy, and this hit his limit. If he'd offended her, he wanted to make good on it. That she was behaving so nonprofessionally pressed a few buttons. He didn't mind mercurial women, but he strongly objected to women who played the gender card just to make guys look bad, and in this, I was with him one hundred percent.

When she showed up at the next rehearsal, Tim confronted her. "Can I speak with you in private?" he asked, his voice low.

She looked at him as if nothing had passed between them. "Sure," she said. "What's up?"

"Susan told me that you thought I

was being inappropriate during rehearsal the other night."

"Oh, that," she said. "Don't worry about it. I was stupid."

He just looked at her, waiting.

"Boyfriend trouble."

He still waited.

"I'm sorry, Tim. I was unfair."

"Apology accepted," he said calmly, and let her go.

TWENTY-NINE

At last, the time had come. It was our final dress rehearsal. If anyone was nervous, it didn't show. The prop people knew what they had to do. The lights were ready, and the stage curtains were in perfect order. Costumes fitted correctly. Lines and movements were memorized. Even the new tiara had come in on time.

We were ready.

I was in the prop area giving a final polish to a desk nameplate when everyone's favorite person walked in.

"No!" I said. "You're not allowed in here!"

One side of his face was still a swollen mess. I had no regrets about that at all.

Randy looked at me and stated what to him was obvious. "Well, how else could I get in?" he asked, pointing to the backstage doors. The ones with the sign on them saying cast and crew only. "The other doors were locked."

I gave him a look of sheer disbelief. "You're not the sharpest spoon in the drawer, are you?"

"Huh?"

"Why are you here anyway?" I'd set the nameplate down in an attempt to thwart myself from ramming it down his throat. The pepper spray was in my shorts pocket.

"To see my girlfriend." He was starting to poke around, touching various things, picking them up, setting them down again, not always in the same place. His fingers roamed aimlessly across the shelves. It was driving me buggy.

Who the heck was his girlfriend?

In any case, there was no time to deal with that issue. I looked at the clock on the wall, heard Peter shout, "Two minutes, people! Two minutes!" The play was about to start, and I had to get this idiot out of here. "Fine," I said, very firmly. "You can go down those stairs—quietly—and take a seat. Don't make a sound. Got it?"

"Yes, ma'am." He winked at me.

I felt nauseous.

As he turned away, he stopped and said one more thing.

"Those curtains of yours almost ruined my utility knives." He smiled smugly.

Wordlessly, I pointed to the seats. He opted for the eighth row left aisle seat.

Marion, on row fifteen, looked at him, looked at me, and nodded. She moved to the same side aisle seat and parked herself directly behind him. Randy turned and smiled at her, and she bowed her head, otherwise ignoring him.

I was still a little stunned. All that had ever been released to the public about the stage curtains was that they'd been vandalized. Not how. Not by what. Everyone there at the time had been sworn to secrecy until such time as the person who did it was caught.

That person had just fallen right into my lap.

I set the nameplate on the desk and went back to the prop room.

Steven arrived with backup six pages into Act I. I'd sent Cam to unlock the front doors and wait for them, but not to interrupt the play. They came in quietly, blocking both aisles.

Randy heard them. He turned, looked, got up and tried to run. Marion helpfully stuck her foot out and tripped him, then got out of the way.

The police were on him in seconds, keeping him on the floor. "Please calm down, Mr. Granger," Steven said. "I really don't want to have to cuff you again. If you will behave yourself, we'll let you up. Are you good with that?"

Randy was. He was confused and angry. "Hey, what'd I do? All I did was come here to watch my girlfriend!"

Peter, his focus torn from the stage, raised his hand to call everything to a halt, and asked, "Sheriff, what are you doing here?" His eyes were dark—he was pissed, and I knew I'd likely catch hell later. I'd broken the sanctity of the uninterrupted dress rehearsal.

"I called them, Peter," I said, my voice as calm as I could make it, even though I was shaking on the inside. It wasn't fear.

"Okay, but why?" His expression told me he knew I was not given to rashness, so must have had a darned good reason. *Phew*, I thought. Our last official dress rehearsal and I was going to live.

I related what Randy had said to me not twenty minutes before.

"Did you say that Mr. Granger?" Steven asked.

By this time, everyone was either onstage or in the seats. Randy had been allowed to stand so long as he kept his hands to himself. He honed in on Corrine, clothes brush in her hand, who was giving him a look of bewilderment and anger. "Hey, Babe, you know this isn't true. You gotta back me up."

"What have you done, Randy?" Her tone was sharp.

I looked at Corrine. "She's your girlfriend? Geez, Corrine, I thought you had better taste." I knew I sounded mean but couldn't help it. "Ask your boyfriend here about when he tried to sexually assault me because I refused his advances one too many times."

Corrine's eyes narrowed. She looked straight at Randy, and he wilted under her glare. "You two-timing little shi—"

"You might also ask him how his face got decorated," I interrupted. Randy's right cheek was indeed colorful. I'd gotten him square on the bone, and even now the point of impact was still a blotch of black and dark purple. It was surrounded by a red corona where I'd managed to break a number of blood vessels. Also, his cheekbone, apparently.

"Damn," Tim said softly. "Remind me never to meet you in a dark alley."

Corrine accessed his bruise. "Did you deck him?" she asked. "Because either way, good on you!" She gave me an approving smile, then turned back to Randy, murder in her eyes. "You lying little creep, you told me you got dragged into a bar brawl!" Guys like Randy didn't lose fights, especially to girls. Except when they did.

"Hey, it was a joke," Randy blurted out, trying to backpedal. "See how much I love you, Babe? How many guys would defe—"

"Shut up," Steven said.

"But she sa—"

"Shut up!" Corrine snapped.

Randy shut.

"Geez, Randy, defend what? What could I possibly need your help defending myself from? I'm glad Joc put you in your place. She saw the real you coming long before I did."

"Speaking of the real you—I said 'No.' Was there something you didn't understand between N and O?"

"Enough," Steven said firmly. "Let's settle this at the station house. Corrine, I think you had better come too." His tone offered that this was not a suggestion. He looked at Peter for some guidance.

Peter sighed. "Okay. Everyone involved in this mess—Corrine, Susan, me, Marian, Joc, Tim, you too Cam, let's go. I'll tell your folks what's going on. Everyone else, work out the rough spots, including any prop issues." He handed his keys to Ed. "Could you lock up tonight? I have no idea how long we'll be, so don't wait up. Try to be out by ten. Thanks, people."

"No one messes with my curtains!"

Marion said as we were leaving.

"Or my players and crew!" Peter added.

Our little entourage stopped at the back of the hall and turned around. Peter called down, "It's looking good, everyone. Yes, we open tomorrow night. You've all done an excellent job and have a lot to be proud of. Well done!" He started to clap.

The rafters rang with applause as we made our exit.

"You should have told me," he replied.

She reached into her purse and took it out, laying it on the table. Such an innocuous thing that had caused so much trouble.

"Thank you," Steven said. "Why is it your fault? Did you cut them?"

"No," she said. "But it's my fault just the same. I let slip I had it to the wrong people." She glared at Randy. "Make that *person*."

"Did you have one made?" Peter asked. "Why?"

She nodded. "At first, I'd been thinking about asking you if I could make one so I could come over on my lunch break and work on costumes, but you were always so busy. Susan and I were having some disagreements about one of her outfits."

"The skirt was too short," Susan said.

"Too much longer and it would have overpowered you onstage," Corrine said, holding her ground. "But we worked it out--"

"I love the new length," Susan interjected.

"—so, I worked on it at home to get the final fitting on the body double, and—"

"Perfect fit, too," Susan said, again standing up for her.

"—and I realized I needed to go to the theater to get some things to finish it, so that's when I came to the school to borrow your key."

"I remember," Peter said. "You said you'd be about an hour and returned it right on time."

"Yes. Well, I got to thinking that it was ridiculous to go through all that trouble, so without asking you, I made a duplicate and returned yours."

"You're probably right about that," Peter said. "The lead costumer should have a key so they can come and go as they need. But why didn't you tell me?"

She looked down. "Well...to tell the truth, I was embarrassed. Felt like I was sneaking around. I was going to give it to you."

"I would have told you to keep it," Peter said. "I just feel stupid for not having thought of it myself. I'm sorry, Corrine."

Corrine looked at him, managed a little nod. "Thank you."

"So, what happened next?" Steven asked.

"And then Randy came over late that night, told me all about Tim, and the next morning, I realized the key had gone missing. When we rehearsed later that night, you and Cam discovered the curtains had been cut." She shook her head. "How could I have been so stupid? I never put it all together until now."

"Mr. Granger," Steven said, his tone slow and deliberate. "Would you care to explain yourself?"

Randy looked at Corrine, tried to smile. "I was helping you," he said.

"*What?*"

"Sure. I mean, after all..."

"Randy, how does stealing a key help me? It was bad enough that I made a copy of it without permission and didn't tell anyone! And you stole it? What the hell were you thinking?"

Peter asked, "What about the curtains?"

"Yes, Randy, do tell," Marion said. Her darlings would be avenged, one way or the other. "What good could you possibly have thought would have come out of ruining them? Why cut them at all?"

"I wanted to give Corrine time."

"Excuse me?" Corrine asked, flummoxed.

"Yeah. Well, Babe, if the curtains weren't there, the show couldn't happen, and if they came down on someone, that might give you the chance to go onstage and—"

She cut him off with a hand, then rubbed her forehead. "Randy, stop. Just stop."

He ignored her. "You're good, Babe, really good." His voice had that awful gooey-cooey baby tone to it, a Daddy-knows-best cadence that made all of us want to hit him.

Corrine took charge. "Who the hell do you think you are to make that choice for me, let alone commit vandalism to prove it?" Her eyes were flashing, her voice low but smoldering with rage. "Did it ever occur to you that if I wanted to act,

I would have auditioned? Did you ever once think about that?" She sat down on the edge of the table, and let out a deep breath, presumably to keep herself from removing certain portions of his anatomy.

"It would be nice to have their replacement cost reimbursed," Marion said, changing the subject. "Including labor. Who will do it, I wonder?" She smiled sweetly at Corrine.

Shooting a dirty look at Randy, Corrine said, "Randy cut them. He will pay for their replacements."

"Hey!" Randy protested, but no one was paying any attention to him.

Marion nodded. "I'm good with that. Peter?"

"Yup," he agreed. "How much were they again, Marion?"

"Let's see," she said slowly, pretending to think it over. She started calculating on her fingers. "New fabric, labor...about one thousand dollars. Each." Her tone was serious, but I could tell she was having great fun making a certain someone extremely nervous.

"What?" Randy exclaimed. "That's not–"

"That is their market value," Marion said, happy to have thrown him for a loop. "However, because I was able to call in some favors, let's just call it seven hundred each, so fourteen hundred total."

"Sounds like a generous offer to me," Steven said. "I'd take it if I were you."

Outnumbered and outmaneuvered, Randy looked down at the floor and mumbled, "How soon do you want it?"

"Not quite done yet," Steven said. "When did you get the key back?"

"I left for work like always, and when

I came home, it was sitting on the kitchen table," Corrine said. "Randy had left. I knew he'd swiped it, but I couldn't prove anything. Just because he stole a key didn't mean he'd wrecked the curtains."

"Agreed," Steven said. "But you are a roofer, Mr. Granger, so obviously heights don't bother you, and had you not just spared us a great deal of trouble by confessing, you still would have been a prime suspect." He paused. "Now. There is still the matter of the rat trap. Was that an accident?"

We all turned to stare at Randy. "Hey!" he said. "Don't look at me! Just because Corrine's a better actor and deserves to be on stage—"

"Randy, Susan makes me look like the rank amateur I am. Not your decision. How dare you harm an innocent person!"

"Hey! I never meant to hurt her, just

scare her!" Randy was yelling now. "I thought she'd see it!"

"In the back of the drawer?" Susan asked, her usually mild demeanor gone. She looked about ready to tenderize him, but Corrine gently laid a hand on her arm.

"Let me," she said, and stepped in front of Randy, her face a mere inch from his. I was surprised he didn't melt in front of her eyes. That look of hers could have turned anyone into goo. "Randy, we are *done*. Okay, so you were a good lay. But you're a total dumbfuck. I never, ever want to see you again. Don't even try. If I want someone to drool all over my décolletage, I'll get a Saint Bernard."

Behind me, I heard Tim start laughing despite himself and try to cover it up with a cough. Steven raised an eyebrow at him. My partner flushed and shook his head. "Sorry," he mouthed.

Ignoring the both of them, Corrine turned to Susan, Peter, and Marion. "You guys, I am so sorry. This all happened because of my stupid *ex*-boyfriend and that damned key and my bad judgement. Susan, can I at least pay the hospital bill?"

"After the insurance," Susan said. "Thank you, honey. That's very nice of you." They hugged.

"Theater people," Steven said, absently scratching his head. "You're all nuts. Don't do it again. Promise me?"

We all raised our right hands and swore.

"Good. Now go home. Not you, Mr. Granger."

THIRTY-ONE

The following night. The theater.
The Princes In The Tower, Act I, Scene

I.

The curtains open.

THE END

ABOUT THE AUTHOR

Cyn Ley has a Master's degree and an interest in just about everything, especially esoteric and off the wall topics. Her more recent occupations include being an author and editor.

Her short stories have been highly praised by critics, some having declared her a master of the genre with well-defined characters and themes that go deep. She is known for writing insightful, intelligent page-turning tales guaranteed to make readers ponder, and which, from time to time, incorporate a strong irreverent streak and sense of the absurd.

So be prepared to think. And laugh. And shudder.

She is the author of BENT DIMENSIONS, a collection of multi-genre short stories; THE SOLACE, an unusual and arresting horror novella; and PILGRIMAGE OF FIRE AND ASH, a coming-of-age short story written for young adults. Her titles are available in print and e-book formats from amazon.com.

She is a lifelong Pacific North-westerner and currently resides in Portland, Oregon, sharing her domicile with a variety of critters.

Cyn is a member of the Northwest Independent Writers Association (NIWA), and a regular contributor to their annual themed anthologies, the most recent being *Guests* (2022),

Harbinger (2023), and *Illusion* (2024).

OTHER TITLES BY CYN LEY

BENT DIMENSIONS

Signs of dimensional drift: possessed carpeting, dolls that aren't, extra "hot" pastries, night stalkers in tin foil hats, soul-searching demons at sci-fi conventions, time loops of life and death and afterlife. The flip side awaits in these engaging tales which resemble reality...until they don't.

THE SOLACE

Living and dead, Ryan's unresting soul has always been in Leah's periphery, and he's never known why. An unusual and arresting tale.

THE PILGRIMAGE OF FIRE AND ASH

On the verge of graduating high school, a budding vulcanologist connects with his future and his soul at Mt. St. Helens.

THIRTY

We gathered in the conference room at the sheriff's office, any other room being too small to hold us all.

"All right," Steven said. "Tell me about the curtains. How did Randy get in?"

"Hey, who says I broke in?" Randy protested.

"You did, Mr. Granger. Now be quiet, please. Was there an extra key?"

"Yes," Corrine said. "It's my fault."

"Do you still have it?" Peter asked.

She nodded. "I was an idiot."